# Contents

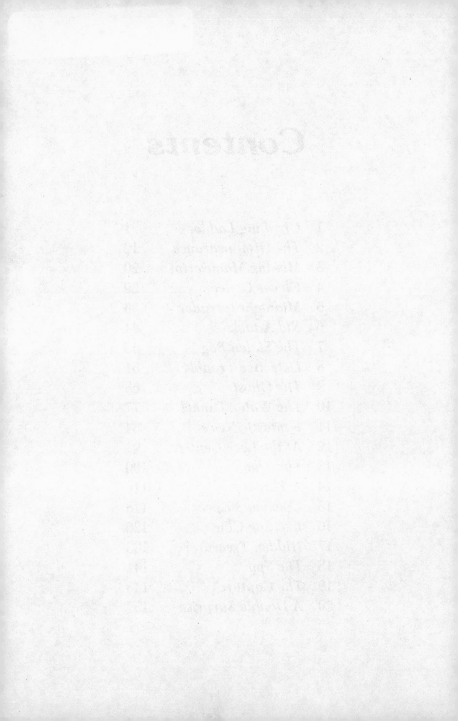

# 1

## Crashing Ladder

"Nancy, what are you doing?" asked Hannah Gruen, pausing at the door of Nancy's bedroom. The attractive, titian-haired girl was seated at her desk writing something hurriedly on a notepad.

"Oh, Hannah," Nancy said, turning around in her chair excitedly, "I've just completed the mystery story for the magazine contest I told you about!"

"That's wonderful, dear," the woman said in a motherly tone. "Now perhaps you can get out and enjoy this lovely weather. You've been cooped up here for days." She went to a window and opened it slightly, allowing a warm breeze to rustle the papers on Nancy's desk.

"For days?" Nancy repeated in mock surprise. "Why, it feels like no time at all." She winked affectionately at the housekeeper who had taken care of her since she was three years old.

"No time, indeed," Hannah said, shaking her head. "You're as pale as the paint on the shutters."

"The old paint or the new paint?" Nancy teased. The pungent odor of a fresh coat of paint drifted through the open window, and they could hear the scraping of a ladder as a man in white overalls worked on the trim.

"It's all the same color," Mrs. Gruen quipped. "Ghost white!"

Nancy smiled. "Aren't you even interested in my solution to the mystery story?"

Hannah slipped her arm around the girl's shoulder. "Of course, I am. May I read it now?"

"Mm-hmm, and you know what?"

"What?"

"I'm going to get lots of sun today."

A smile crossed Hannah's lips as she glanced at the penciled page half hidden by several others. "I must confess, Nancy, I'm very happy about this mystery."

"You are?"

"Yes, because it's one you were able to solve in the safety of your own home!"

"Oh, Hannah . . ." Nancy laughed. Although she

was eighteen years old now and well-known as a capable amateur detective, she knew Hannah could not help worrying about her.

Without another word, the girl put the papers in order and clipped them together. "Here you are," she said, handing the manuscript to Hannah.

"Let me get my reading glasses," Hannah said, excusing herself just when the front doorbell rang.

"That must be Bess and George," Nancy said. "I called them while you were out shopping." She dropped the papers on her desk and flew down the stairs, followed by Hannah. "Hi!" She welcomed the visitors. Bess Marvin and her cousin George Fayne were Nancy's closest friends.

"Have you come to rescue the fair maiden from her ivory tower?" Hannah said mischievously.

"Guess so," Bess smiled, revealing deep dimples in her cheeks. "We're taking Nancy to Pickles and Plums for lunch!"

The Drews' housekeeper wrinkled her nose. "Are you sure you won't get indigestion on that diet?" she asked innocently.

"Oh, no!" George giggled. "It's a new health-food restaurant downtown. We can sit outside and get lots of vitamins A and D."

Hannah's eyes brightened. "Health food! That sounds just like what the doctor ordered," she said approvingly.

3

Nancy kissed the woman's cheek, then ran upstairs, calling to her friends, "C'mon, I want to show you the story I'm submitting to *Circle and Square* magazine!"

"Can't we eat first?" Bess replied, following her cousin to the second landing. "I'm starved!"

"So what else is new?" George teased. Unlike Bess, who tended to be plump, George had a slim figure.

"I haven't eaten a thing today! Really!" Bess giggled as Nancy gave her the manuscript to read.

"Let me see it too," George said eagerly. "I want to learn what happened to the mystery man."

"Just a minute," Bess protested, holding the manuscript away from her cousin and toward the sunlight streaming through the bedroom window.

"Oh, please don't keep me in suspense," George begged.

"For all those terrible things you always say about my figure," Bess declared, "you'll have to wait your turn."

George shrugged. "Beaten again."

"Who's beaten—someone in your manuscript?" Hannah Gruen interrupted, joining the girls.

"No, no." Nancy chuckled. "This is a love story. Actually, it won't make much sense unless I tell you how the whole thing started. The opening of the story appeared in the magazine. It contains a

4

real-life mystery which every contest entrant is supposed to solve."

As Nancy spoke, Hannah sat in the Queen Anne chair opposite the girl's desk while Bess and George plopped at the foot of the bed.

"I gather from the little I read," Bess put in, "that the story takes place in Europe."

"That's right," Nancy replied. "It starts in Brussels, Belgium, in the nineteenth century. A handsome young man whose name was François Lefèvre received a pair of mysterious lace cuffs which he wore with a red velvet dress jacket."

Bess leaned forward with a starry look. "Mm, too bad he isn't living now. I'd love to meet him."

"Believe me," Nancy said, "you would have been only one of many admirers. One of them apparently was too bashful to tell him how much she cared for him."

"You mean he never found out who sent him the lace cuffs?" George asked.

Nancy nodded. "François disappeared suddenly with a rather sizable fortune. Neither his family nor friends ever heard from him again."

"Oh, how sad!" Bess remarked.

"In the fireplace of his bedroom," Nancy continued, "his servants found burned fragments of letters. Among them was a mysterious note in flowery handwriting—"

"Obviously from a woman." George seized the clue.

"It was in French," Nancy said. "Translated the message read:

> Turn your face
> To the lace
> Of the cuffs
> A secret—

The rest of it was charred."

"Did the servants find anything else?" Hannah questioned eagerly.

"Yes, on another shred of paper was the word *marry*."

"What a story," Bess said dreamily.

"Does anyone know who sent the lace cuffs to François?" George inquired.

"The story didn't say," Nancy replied. "I guess no one ever admitted to being the lace maker."

"Oh, please tell us the rest," Bess said, "before you hear my news—"

Nancy's eyebrows shot up. "What news?"

"We'll get to that later. Finish your story first."

"Well, what I've told you so far is all that was published in the magazine. Everything else I made up."

Nancy handed the housekeeper her story. "Hannah's first. I promised to let her see it before you arrived."

The woman began reading the manuscript with great interest. Bess was quiet for a while, then became impatient. "Nancy, got your passport ready?" she asked.

"Why, where are we going?"

"To Belgium!" Bess blurted.

"Belgium?" Nancy said in puzzlement. "Now, Bess, I told you François Lefèvre has been dead for more than a century."

Grinning, Bess swept a blond curl off her forehead. "We're not going there to hunt for François," she said. "You remember my telling you about Mother's old college friend, Madame Chambray?"

Nancy nodded.

"Well, about a month ago she moved from France to Brugge, Belgium—"

"Why, that's the name of a city in Nancy's story," Hannah interrupted.

"You're kidding," Bess said.

"No, it's true," Nancy concurred, "but tell me about Madame Chambray."

"She wrote to Mother recently. Here's the letter," Bess said, rummaging through her purse for it. "It seems that Madame Chambray found a valuable antique cross in her house. It's made of diamonds and lapis lazuli. Madame Chambray believes it belongs to someone who lived in her house years ago. Unfortunately, she hasn't had

7

much time to search for the owner of the cross but she's going to put an ad in the newspaper over there."

Intrigued by the story, Nancy glanced at the letter for a moment, then dropped it on the desk. "What about the person from whom Madame Chambray bought the house?" the girl detective inquired. "Isn't it more likely the cross belongs to him or her?"

"Apparently it doesn't," George spoke up. "Madame Chambray checked on that."

Just then Hannah, not taking her eyes from the manuscript, commented, "It's a wonderful story, dear. You know, I'd been hoping you'd be content to work on fictional mysteries for a while, but I can see—"

Before the housekeeper could continue, there was the shatter of glass followed by an earsplitting crash.

"Oh, my goodness!" Hannah shrieked, rushing to the window.

"What was it?" the girls chorused as they ran after her.

"The painter!" Hannah cried. "His ladder must have slipped and he fell!"

All four were staring down at the lawn, where the man in white overalls was dizzily swaying to his feet. The ladder was lying on the grass a few feet away from him.

8

"I hope he isn't badly hurt," Hannah said. "We'd better go down and find out."

Her words were hardly spoken, when the man quickly hobbled across the lawn to a truck parked in front of the Drew home. Nancy raced downstairs two steps at a time, the others close behind her, and bolted outside along the curving driveway toward the truck.

"Are you okay?" she shouted anxiously to the man.

But he pulled himself into the driver's seat, slammed the door, and roared off. Nancy turned back to the house, meeting her friends and Hannah halfway. The housekeeper still held the manuscript in her hand.

"The ladder must've slid straight down," Mrs. Gruen observed, "and hit the dining room window."

Nancy gaped at the pile of broken glass beneath the opening. "I'm going to call the paint company immediately," she announced.

"That guy sure acted strange, don't you think?" Bess said.

"I just hope he's all right," Hannah said.

Nancy dialed the phone number of the painters, Kell and Kell, and talked with the owner, Oscar Kell. He offered to come at once to see the damage. While they waited, Nancy and the other girls decided to take a second look at the scene themselves.

"Be careful," George cautioned Nancy as she walked gingerly between shards of broken glass.

"What do you think of this?" Nancy said, ignoring her friend's comment. She pointed to a paint can standing on the ground a few feet away from the window.

"It's white paint," Bess said. "What are you getting at?"

"If he was working on my window frame, the can would have fallen and splattered paint on the grass, wouldn't it?" Nancy questioned.

"You're right," George admitted. "He climbed up there without it. I wonder why he did that?"

"I have a hunch he was eavesdropping on us!"

# 2

## The Disappearance

"How much do you think the painter overheard?" Bess asked after Nancy revealed her conclusions.

"Probably only snatches," Nancy replied, "but enough to give him ideas."

"Well, I wouldn't worry too much about it," George said. "He didn't find out your solution to the contest."

"True, but I bet he wanted to," Nancy replied. "He must have heard us talking about the mystery while he was painting near the window. So he scooted down his ladder and moved it right underneath my room, and climbed up again. Of course, by doing that, he missed part of the conversation."

George nodded. "He probably mixed everything

up and figures there's some important connection between your contest and Madame Chambray's story!"

As George spoke, a station wagon pulled into the driveway. A middle-aged man with stocky features emerged. "I'm looking for Nancy Drew," he called to the girls.

Nancy stepped forward. "Mr. Kell?"

"That's me," he said, knitting his eyebrows as he noticed the broken window. "I'm sorry I couldn't get over here faster. I was waiting for Matey to return with the truck."

"Did he?" Nancy asked impatiently.

"Yep, and before I could find out what happened, he quit on me. Said he was tired of house painting. When I asked him what he intended to do, he said he was going treasure hunting. A real smart aleck!"

Nancy, unwilling to reveal her suspicions, innocently asked, "What's his last name?"

"Johnson," Mr. Kell replied. "He used to be a sailor; I guess climbing the mast was good training for the kind of work he did for me."

"Was he with you a long time?" Nancy asked.

"A year. He's been on parole for a while," Mr. Kell said with hesitation in his voice. "But he's okay. A good painter, just a smart aleck."

Bess and George had all they could do to contain their anxiety while Nancy spoke to Mr. Kell. Then

Hannah appeared at the dining room window, and for several moments she and the contractor discussed repairs.

When he left, Bess grabbed Nancy's arm. "I don't believe it!" she said. "That painter is an ex-convict!"

"Matey Johnson was probably a second-story burglar," Nancy concluded.

"To think he could've just squirmed his way into your room and stolen your manuscript!" George exclaimed.

"But he didn't," Nancy pointed out calmly. "Of course, if he had, he could've copied my answer to the contest and sent it in. Then, if his entry had reached the magazine office first, the editors would have accused me of plagiarism."

"How awful!" George said. "But he would have been the plagiarist—the one who stole your idea!"

"I know," Nancy said, "but how could I prove it?"

"We're your witnesses," Bess said cheerfully.

"You're more than witnesses." Nancy smiled. "You're my best friends."

"Say, what about lunch?" George piped up.

"Don't tell us you're hungry!" Her cousin smirked.

The girls went to get their handbags. Nancy saw the manuscript lying in the hallway where Hannah had placed it after she had come back into the house. Quickly the girl put it into the closet before she followed her friends outside.

They climbed into Nancy's car and headed for Pickles and Plums Restaurant. Outside were rows of round yellow tables with floral umbrellas poised in the center of each one. Several of the umbrellas were open; a few were not.

"Let's get a little sun," Nancy suggested, remembering her promise to Hannah.

The girls chose a table with a closed umbrella and within a minute or so a lanky waiter in blue jeans and a floral shirt brought them menus.

As soon as Bess had ordered an exotic fruit and yogurt salad, she leaned toward Nancy. "We never did read the rest of your story so please tell us how it ends."

Nancy said she felt sure there was a message in the lace cuffs that prompted François to disappear.

"What kind of message?" Bess persisted.

"I have a strong hunch that the girl who made the cuffs was in love with François but he didn't love her. Maybe he was fearful his family and the girl's would arrange their betrothal. In those days young people had little to say about such things."

"How horrible!" George spoke up.

"I understand that marriages are still arranged in some countries," Nancy said.

"Well, I'm glad I don't live in one of them," George declared.

Bess saw a chance to tease her cousin. "I'm sure Burt is equally happy about it," she commented.

In reply George wrinkled up her nose. Burt Eddleton was her favorite date.

"Of course," Nancy said, interrupting the banter between her friends, "I don't think François ever left Belgium."

"What!" Bess and George said. They were totally bewildered.

"But the story said he disappeared," George noted.

"He did—from Brussels. But I have a hunch he stayed in his native country. You see, he was very interested in painting. I didn't mention this earlier, but he always wanted to study with Dirk Gelder, a famous teacher in nineteenth-century Brugge. I think François might have gone there."

"But that's not far from Brussels," George objected.

"I know. Yet, in those days people didn't travel as they do now. If he changed his appearance a little and learned how to speak the dialect of that town, he could conceal himself easily enough."

"Don't they speak Flemish there?" Bess inquired.

"Flemish is spoken in Flanders," Nancy ad-

16

mitted. "But the people in Brugge have their own dialect."

As the chatter continued, the lanky waiter placed three large platters of salad in front of the girls.

"You said that François took a fortune with him when he left," George put in. "In those days robberies were as prevalent as today. Did it occur to you that maybe he was overtaken and killed?"

Nancy admitted the thought had entered her mind. "But the magazine story doesn't even hint at foul play. My impression is that François changed his whole appearance and life-style. He could've grown a beard to hide his handsome face and switched to plain clothes, for instance."

"In your story," Bess asked, "what name did he take?"

"Karl Van Pelt."

"I still think it's incredible," George insisted, "that such an attractive man could live no more than sixty miles from Brussels without ever being identified. His clothes alone—"

"Not really," Nancy interrupted. "Don't forget, according to the magazine, he took no clothes other than the red jacket with the lace cuffs. Obviously, he didn't want to be seen with any baggage to indicate he was traveling or moving away. He could've hidden whatever treasure he had in his sleeves, pockets, and shoes and rolled up the jacket into a neat little package."

"In that case," George pointed out, "François's personal fortune must've been in money and jewels."

Nancy nodded. "Exactly. In my story I said he used some of the money to start a successful business and at his death willed the red jacket to a museum."

"Just think," Bess said, digging her fork into a cube of fresh melon, "we'll be able to walk on the same cobblestones François did and look at the same canals he saw and—"

George rolled her eyes upward in mock disgust. "Spare me," she said. "I don't know how Dave stands it." Dave Evans was Bess's boyfriend.

"Okay, you two," Nancy broke in.

"You know I was serious about us all going to Belgium," Bess said. "Madame Chambray has plenty of room and more than one mystery to solve!"

"Really?" Nancy asked eagerly.

"Yes. She found part of an old letter too, which says something about a treasure."

"Is that all she said?"

Bess nodded. "Madame Chambray didn't reveal too many details in her letter to my mother, but she does want us—you especially—to visit. She

18

knows your dad's a lawyer and that you often solve mysteries."

Nancy's heart was beating excitedly. "I'm just flabbergasted," she said. "After working on the mystery contest, the one place I'm eager to see is Brugge!"

"Who knows, maybe we'll find François's red jacket in one of the museums!" George giggled.

"Let's not get too carried away," Nancy said. "After all, my part of the story is only fictional. Speaking of that, I ought to mail it in at once."

George called to the waiter for a bill as Nancy caught sight of someone bending behind the front fender of her parked car. "Is he letting the air out of my tire?" she cried, pushing her chair back and darting toward him. "What do you think you're doing?" she shouted.

For a split second the stranger bobbed into view. He looked like Matey Johnson!

# 3

## Missing Manuscript

"Stop!" Nancy cried, dashing into the street after the man. But he darted away lithe as a cat, skirting several taxis and bike riders before disappearing into an alley.

Stymied by the heavy traffic, Nancy did not attempt to cross the street. George and Bess, who had quickly paid the waiter, were now staring at the front right wheel of Nancy's car. The tire was slowly going flat!

"What a shame!" Bess remarked.

"Who was that guy anyway?" George asked.

"I'm pretty sure it was Matey Johnson. I didn't get much of a look at him at the house but I recognized his reddish-blond hair."

While Nancy removed a tire inflator from her trunk and hooked it to the wheel, she listened quietly as her friends discussed the latest event.

"Why would Matey Johnson let air out of Nancy's tire?" Bess asked her cousin.

"Obviously he wanted to stall us here for a while," George said.

"Well, he sure accomplished that," Nancy sighed, watching the air-pressure gauge slowly creep higher.

"You don't suppose," Bess suggested, "that he's planning to go back to your house?"

"That's exactly what I was thinking," Nancy said. "If only I could speed up the air pump!"

At last the tire was mended. "Keep an eye on everything," the girl detective told the cousins. "I'm going to phone Hannah."

Nancy disappeared into the restaurant again to use the public telephone. In less than five minutes she returned with a glum expression on her face.

"What's the matter?" Bess asked.

"Nobody's home."

"Uh-oh," George commented. Then, out of the corner of her eye, she noticed a River Heights patrol car cruising toward them. "Isn't that Chief McGinnis?" she said.

Nancy waved frantically to him, calling at the same time, "Chief! Chief McGinnis!"

The young police officer at the wheel swung the car behind Nancy's and his superior stepped out.

"What happened?" Chief McGinnis inquired, gazing at the tire. "Did you pick up a nail?"

Quickly Nancy explained, adding her fear that Matey Johnson might be on his way to her house to steal something important.

"In that case," the chief said, nodding to the other policeman, "you stay here with the girls. I'll drive Nancy home."

Nancy gave George the keys to her car and slipped her registration in the glove compartment. When she and Chief McGinnis presently pulled into her driveway, the girl flew to the front door past the ladder which was now standing up against the house again. She fumbled for her key, opened the door, and ran upstairs.

"It's gone!" she exclaimed. "Oh, Chief, the letter I told you about is gone!"

"Are you sure?" the man replied as he reached the landing.

Nancy sorted nervously through numerous papers on her desk, opened all the drawers, and peered behind and under the furniture. There was no sign of Madam Chambray's letter.

"What about your manuscript?" the police chief said.

"Oh, I put that in the hall closet," Nancy said.

"Let me check." She hurried downstairs and opened the closet door.

"Oh, good!" she cried out. "It's still here!"

Chief McGinnis had followed her. "The thief couldn't find it," he deduced.

Nancy nodded. "Matey Johnson must have looked for it in my room. But Hannah brought it down here and I put it away before we went out to lunch."

"Nancy," the police officer said, "I'd like to caution you about one thing. Even though you saw Johnson deflating your tire, you don't have any proof he burglarized this house."

The girl detective agreed. "But I have an idea. The ladder you saw downstairs was moved by somebody. I'm going to check it for fingerprints. If they all belong to Matey—"

Her voice faded as she took a fingerprint kit from a desk drawer and went outside with the chief.

"You know, Nancy," he said, smiling, "I don't think I've ever watched you lift fingerprints!"

"Any chance I can work on the force?" Nancy said impishly, removing a can of spray powder from the kit.

"Just let me know when you're ready!"

The young detective dusted parts of the ladder with powder, then pressed rubberized lifting tape over the latent prints. She peeled off the tape with the powder on it, and sealed the impressions under a plastic cover.

"Would you identify these for me?" she asked.

"As soon as I get back to headquarters," the chief promised.

He backed the patrol car out of the driveway as Bess and George pulled up at the curb.

"Is everything okay?" Bess asked, darting across the lawn ahead of her cousin.

"I'm afraid not," Nancy said grimly. "The letter Madame Chambray sent your mother is missing and I'm practically certain Matey Johnson stole it. I'm waiting for Chief McGinnis to identify some fingerprints for me."

Bess and George were stunned. "What about your manuscript?" George asked. "Was that taken too?"

"Fortunately, no," the young detective said, "and before anything does happen to it, I'd better type up the final draft and mail it to *Circle and Square* magazine."

"This is really exciting," Bess remarked, giving her friend an enthusiastic hug. "I hope you win first prize!"

"Thanks," Nancy said appreciatively. "The magazine is awarding a large cash prize which I'd like to donate to charity."

After Nancy had typed the story and labeled the

24

precious package, the girls drove to the River Heights post office, where Nancy then suggested they speak to Mr. Kell. "I'd like to get Matey Johnson's address from him."

"You're not planning to visit Matey, are you?" Bess inquired nervously.

"I might," Nancy said and aimed the car toward a small industrial park at the edge of town.

Kell and Kell proved to be a fairly large company with an attractive office. When Nancy greeted the young woman behind the desk and asked to see the owner, the receptionist giggled.

"Oh, you're Nancy Drew. How I envy you trotting around the world and solving mysteries! Do they always start with something simple like a falling ladder?"

Nancy and the other girls laughed. "It's not that simple," Nancy replied.

"But just as startling," Bess added, as the receptionist announced the visitors to Mr. Kell.

Momentarily, he stepped out of an inner office. "No more trouble, I hope," he said warily.

The young detective bit her lip, not wishing to say anything in front of the receptionist. "May we talk to you privately?" she asked.

"Certainly."

As concisely as she could, Nancy told him what had happened that afternoon. "Would you please give me Mr. Johnson's address?" she requested.

"He was staying at a friend's apartment while he worked here," Mr. Kell said. "As a matter of fact, his friend—André Bergère—worked here a few years ago; a real loner and not too friendly to the other people in the shop."

He buzzed the receptionist for the address. It was in a section of River Heights where many European people lived.

"Are you game to go?" Nancy turned to her friends.

"I guess so," Bess said reluctantly, "but I don't relish meeting either André or Matey face to face."

When the girls arrived at the address, neither name was listed in the lobby directory. Bess was relieved. "Well, that settles that," she stated. "Let's go home."

"Not yet," Nancy replied. She decided to knock at the door of a tenant on the first floor. An elderly man answered. "Would you happen to know if a Mr. André Bergère lives here?" she asked.

"No, he doesn't. Moved out a little while ago."

"Did he say where he was going?" George pressed the man.

"I think he said Europe."

"That's very interesting," Bess commented. "You don't suppose he went to Belgium?"

The elderly tenant shrugged. "I have no idea," he replied. "Sorry I can't be of further help to you girls."

"Now what?" George asked.

Nancy said she wanted to discuss everything with her father the next evening, when he was due to return from a business trip.

"Well, don't solve the mystery before we all see each other again!" Bess exclaimed as she and George parted to do errands.

"Don't worry," Nancy said lightly. "There's no chance of it!"

The trio said good-bye in the center of the shopping district. Nancy returned home to find Hannah knitting a sweater and waiting for a cake to finish baking in the oven.

"Something smells delicious," Nancy remarked.

"Your favorite—angel food cake." The housekeeper smiled. "I thought you deserved a little special dessert to celebrate the completion of your manuscript."

"Oh, Hannah, you're such a dear. You always do something to make me feel better."

That evening Nancy went to bed early. She wondered if her priority mail package would reach the magazine office quickly, as promised. What if someone intercepts it? she thought anxiously, then chided herself. Oh, that's silly. Why would anybody—

She drifted off to sleep, but late the next morning she could not resist calling *Circle and Square* to find out if her entry had been received. The young woman on the other end of the line was rather curt. "Entries haven't been sorted yet," she said flatly. "Call back later, miss." She hung up.

To Nancy's chagrin, the answer was equally disappointing that afternoon. The manuscript had not arrived so she made a beeline to the post office.

The clerk on duty offered to put a tracer on the package. "Stop back in a few days," he suggested.

But the contest deadline is tomorrow, Nancy thought desperately. What am I going to do?

Nancy rushed to her father's law office and with the help of his secretary, Miss Hanson, she made photocopies of her carbon copy of the manuscript. Then, taking a chance her Aunt Eloise, who lived in New York City, would be able to hand-deliver it to the magazine, she returned to the post office.

"This package must reach New York tomorrow," Nancy said, "so please send it the fastest way possible."

"I can't promise there is a fastest way," the clerk said. "There's a transit strike in New York, and mail trucks are having a tough time getting through."

"Oh, dear," Nancy replied worriedly.

What if the second copy of her manuscript did not reach *Circle and Square* magazine the next day? She would lose her chance to enter the contest!

# 4

## Clever Caller

Seeing the glum expression in Nancy's eyes, the postal clerk added cheerfully, " 'Course express mail usually gets through no matter what."

Nancy sighed. "I hope so."

That evening before her father arrived home, she telephoned his sister. "Aunt Eloise, would you mind doing me a very special favor?" the young sleuth requested.

"I'd be glad to. Just tell me what it is," Miss Drew replied.

Briefly Nancy told her about the manuscript, how the first copy had gone astray and that she had mailed Aunt Eloise a second copy to be hand-delivered. "I hate to trouble you with this in the midst of a transit strike," Nancy apologized, "but the magazine office is not too far from your apartment. Do you mind very much?"

"Now don't be silly. Of course not," the kindly woman answered. "I wish you could come for a visit. It's been so long since I've seen you, Nancy."

Her niece promised that she would try to spend a weekend in New York soon. "And I'll bring my bike!" she added with a chuckle.

When Carson Drew arrived home later that evening, Nancy was eager to tell him about the recent events at the Drew house. One by one she related all of the problems.

"Don't worry about your manuscript," the tall, distinguished-looking man consoled her. "Your Aunt Eloise will see that your package gets to the proper person."

"I'm sure, Dad," Nancy said. "It's just that—"

"Winning the contest isn't everything, you know," Mr. Drew interrupted. Nancy began to smile as he continued. "I've been doing some serious thinking, Nancy. And in view of everything you've told me, I think you ought to consider some on-the-spot investigation."

"Oh, Dad, do you mean it?" Nancy burst out joyfully.

"Sure I mean it."

The girl threw her arms around her father, hugging him happily. "Bess invited George and me to stay at Madame Chambray's!" she exclaimed and hurried to the telephone.

By next morning the three friends had chatted several times, discussed travel arrangements and clothes, and made a long-distance call to Madame Chambray.

After breakfast, the telephone rang again. This time it was Aunt Eloise Drew.

"Good news, dear," she reported to Nancy. "Your manuscript arrived and I took it immediately to the magazine office."

"Oh, wonderful," Nancy said.

"Well, not entirely." Miss Drew's voice became somber. "I asked to see Mr. Miller, the editor-in-chief of the company, but before the receptionist could buzz his office, another man rushed up to me and said, 'You have Nancy Drew's manuscript? I'll take it.' Of course, I wouldn't give it to him. He was rather unpleasant about it, and I really was afraid we'd come to verbal blows."

"Oh, dear," Nancy said. "Who was he?"

"I don't know. Fortunately, though, Mr. Miller appeared. The receptionist told him I was delivering the second copy of your story because the first entry had been lost en route."

Nancy fastened on every word. "What did the other man do?" she asked.

31

"Well, Mr. Miller turned to him and said, 'You're not connected with this contest, are you, Mr. Rocke?' Rocke said he wasn't, and that he had merely offered to take the package to the proper person. To tell the truth, Nancy, he gave me an uneasy feeling. I insisted that Mr. Miller look after your entry personally."

"Thank you so much, Aunt Eloise," Nancy said gratefully. "You're a real lifesaver."

After hanging up, Nancy related the conversation to Hannah Gruen, then called her father at his office. He was as puzzled as Nancy. "I can't imagine why there is so much interest in your manuscript," Mr. Drew commented. "It's only a magazine contest."

"That's what I thought, Dad," Nancy said.

Deciding to put her aunt's strange encounter out of her mind, Nancy headed downtown to do some shopping for her trip. On the way, though, she suddenly remembered that she had not heard from Chief McGinnis and stopped at police headquarters.

"I should've called you yesterday," the chief apologized, "but I got bogged down on a couple of things. Those prints do belong to Matey Johnson, so it looks as if he stole that letter from you. Even so, you might have a hard time proving it. I'm waiting for him to report to his parole officer."

"He probably won't," Nancy said and told about

her trip to the apartment house where he no longer lived. "I should've mentioned this as soon as I found out. But I've been worried about sending my manuscript to the magazine and now I'm leaving for Europe."

"Well, have a wonderful trip—"

"It should be a mysterious one," Nancy interrupted, reminding Chief McGinnis about Madame Chambray's story of the antique cross and its missing owner.

After leaving police headquarters, she made a few purchases, including a pretty blue sweater-coat that matched the color of her eyes, then returned home. To her delight, Hannah said Ned Nickerson had called. He and Nancy were special friends; neither of them ever dated anyone else. For a moment a picture of the tall, good-looking athlete from Emerson College swept pleasantly across her mind.

"Nancy," Mrs. Gruen said, interrupting the girl's daydream, "poor Ned has laryngitis. He could hardly talk but he wanted to know how you were and what you were doing. When I told him you were flying to Belgium with Bess and George to solve a mystery, he sounded very downhearted and said he wished he could go along."

"I wish he could too," said Nancy, "but he has a summer job I know he can't leave."

Eager to speak to him herself, Nancy dialed his

number. To her amazement Ned's voice was clear as a bell. He said he certainly had not phoned her!

Fear suddenly rippled through her as she revealed her travel plans. "Then Hannah told a stranger about Bess, George, and me definitely going to Belgium in connection with a mystery."

"That's bad," Ned remarked. "I'm sorry I won't be able to come along to protect you, but I just can't get away right now. I'll see you before you go, won't I?"

"I don't know," Nancy said. "We're leaving as soon as we get our reservations." She admitted she was glad Hannah had not been aware of the details of her flight. "So your impersonator didn't find out anything definite about our departure."

Ned agreed. "But when you find out what flight you're taking, please tell me. Promise?"

"Promise." Nancy blushed.

With so many chores to finish before leaving, the rest of the day flew by. At bedtime she crawled between the covers, checking off in her mind all that was left to do. Then, yawning deeply, she fell asleep.

A strange clipping sound awakened her a few hours later. She listened intently. The noise stopped. Was she dreaming? Nancy closed her eyes again, telling herself to ignore the interruption. Then *clip, clip, clip*.

What is that sound? she wondered, lifting her head off the pillow. She squinted at the open window across the room where a shadowy face was outlined in the moonlight.

A man was cutting the screen with a large pair of shears!

# 5

## Midnight Intruder

Nancy's heart pounded as she watched the blades sink through the screen wire. Desperately she wondered what to do. If she slammed the window down and locked it, the intruder could not enter her room.

But then he'd escape for sure, Nancy decided, and come back another time when I wasn't here to catch him!

Quietly she got out of bed and tiptoed to her father's room.

"Dad!" she whispered hoarsely. "Dad! Wake up! Someone's trying to break into my room!"

Mr. Drew stirred uneasily, mumbling in reply.

"Dad!" Nancy repeated nervously as he blinked

his eyes open. "A burglar is breaking into the house!"

"Where is he?" her father asked. Now fully awake, he followed Nancy back to her room.

There, staring at the girl's empty bed, stood the intruder! Instantly, Mr. Drew pounced on the man, throwing him to the floor. He pinned his arms back to prevent him from pulling out a weapon.

"Let me go!" the stranger bellowed. He tried to wriggle out from under his captor. But Mr. Drew sat squarely on his chest!

"Call the police, Nancy!" her father said, glaring at his prisoner.

The girl detective was already dialing headquarters. She told the sergeant on duty what had happened. "Please hurry over here," she said, ending the conversation. Then she turned to her father. "They're sending two policemen right away."

Once more the captive struggled for release. He pushed his knees up and dug his feet into the plush carpet, trying to get a strong foothold.

"No, you don't," Nancy informed him, forcing his knees down and sitting on them.

"Ou-ouch!" he cried out furiously. "Get off me. You're breaking my bones!"

The rumpus in the room carried into the adjacent one where Hannah Gruen slept. She awoke

and rushed to the scene. Flipping on the overhead light, she gasped. "Oh, my goodness! Who is he?"

"You're Matey Johnson, aren't you?" Nancy responded as she leaned back and noticed the man's reddish-blond hair.

All color drained from his face. His mouth quivered open but shut quickly.

"Well, when the police get here—" Nancy began as the front doorbell rang.

Hannah hurried downstairs. Shortly two officers appeared in the girl's room and immediately handcuffed the prisoner. After advising him of his legal rights, one of the policemen said, "Haven't I seen you around the station?"

The captive tightened his lips angrily.

"This is Matey Johnson." Nancy identified him. "He's been out on parole."

"How do you know th—" the intruder began, then caught himself.

"Why were you trying to break into our house?" Nancy questioned. "You already stole Mrs. Marvin's letter. Were you coming back for my manuscript?"

Matey refused to answer.

"And I suppose," the girl detective went on, "that paint ladder came in handy again, didn't it?"

She pulled a flashlight from her desk drawer and shone it out the damaged window. Sure enough, the ladder was leaning against the house!

"Too bad we didn't think of putting it in the garage," the girl said to her father.

"You're right," Mr. Drew admitted. "We made it easy for Johnson to break in a second time. Only this time he didn't get away with it!"

Johnson glowered as the officers led him out of the house. Hannah Gruen locked the door behind them and yawned. "What a night!" she said.

Nancy nodded. "You know, I'm hungry all of a sudden. Would anyone else like a snack?"

Mr. Drew laughed, following Hannah and his daughter into the kitchen. "I guess I lost a few calories sitting on that character! How about another dish of your rice pudding, Hannah?"

"Coming right up," she said. "I think we all need to eat a little something to settle our nerves." She dished out the rice pudding while Nancy made cups of steaming hot chocolate topped with whipped cream.

"It's too bad you didn't get your letter back from Mr. Johnson," the attorney said to his daughter.

She shrugged, spooning a bit of the cream into her mouth. "I'm just glad we caught him," she said. "The only thing that bothers me is he may have shown the letter to someone else—like André Bergère."

The next morning Nancy told Bess and George all about the midnight intruder and her father's bravery.

"It sounds to me you were pretty courageous yourself," Bess complimented her friend. "I would have been totally paralyzed!"

"Oh, that isn't true," Nancy remarked. "You've been in lots of scary situations with me and done okay."

Bess giggled in embarrassment. "I'm hoping, though, there won't be any in Belgium," she said, leading Nancy to reveal Hannah Gruen's phone conversation with Ned's impersonator. "Oh, no!" Bess panicked. "Maybe we ought to give up the trip!"

"No, indeed," the girl detective replied, "but if *you* want to back out—"

"Oh, I'll go along," Bess agreed reluctantly, "but I know I'll be a wreck the whole time."

George's reaction was quite different. The minute she heard Nancy's story she said, "The sooner we leave the U.S.A. the better off we'll all be!"

"I hope you're right," Nancy commented, "but we might just run into trouble in Belgium."

"You mean we might run into Bergère," George said, adding crisply, "Well, let's talk about something more pleasant. Burt says he, Dave, and Ned want to come here tomorrow to say good-bye. Since we only have a short time left before our trip—"

"Listen," Nancy interrupted, "I want everybody to have dinner here, all right?"

"Fabulous," George replied.

The girls contacted their Emerson friends at once. When the boys arrived the next evening, Dave suggested going to a local show followed by a dance to benefit a home for handicapped children.

Dave, who had driven Burt and Ned to the Drew house, chided himself for not thinking ahead. "I am really stupid," he said. "There are six of us, but my car can only take four."

"That's okay," Nancy said. "Ned and I can use my car."

The three couples drove off in two cars, but Dave and Ned did not follow the same route. Bess, George, and their escorts arrived first. They waited in the lobby for Nancy and Ned.

"I wonder where they are," Burt remarked after a while, glancing impatiently at his watch. "We've been here almost fifteen minutes. Did Nancy say anything about stopping on the way?"

"No," George answered.

She and the others watched the last trickle of audience take their seats. "It's curtain time," Dave commented. "Maybe we should go inside."

"What do you think, George?" Bess asked. "You know it's not like Nancy to be late. I hope nothing has happened to them."

The sound of applause now drifted through the

doors into the lobby which, except for the four-some, was empty. "Oh, I'm sure they'll be here soon," George said, leading the way into the darkened auditorium.

On stage was a beautiful woman with long silky hair that hung over the shoulders of her white sequined gown. She began to sing softly, bringing a hush over the auditorium. Bess, however, could not concentrate on the performance, that featured several popular songs including a romantic ballad she loved. Bess bit her lips anxiously and turned her head now and then to look at the closed doors.

"What's the matter?" Dave whispered to his date, putting his hand comfortingly on hers.

"I have a feeling something dreadful has happened to Nancy and Ned!" Bess answered in alarm.

# 6

## Kid Attack

Nancy and Ned had started to follow Dave's car but soon realized another one was tailing theirs. Its headlights created a glare in Nancy's rearview mirror which caused Ned, who was driving, to push the mirror back.

"At the next side street," Ned said, "I'll turn right and switch off the headlights. If the car passes us, we can stop worrying."

Nancy stared out the back window trying to see who was in the vehicle, but could not discern anyone's face. Ned pressed down on the accelerator and screeched around the corner, switching off his lights as he swung past a truck and swerved over to the curb in front of a parked car.

44

"I think we lost them," the young man said, pulling onto the road again.

"We can get back to the main street by turning at the end of this one," Nancy observed. But suddenly a roadblock of wooden sawhorses came into view. A sign attached to them read:

BRIDGE OUT. ROAD CLOSED.
WATER AHEAD. DANGER!

"Sorry," Nancy said to her friend. "I guess the old twenty-twenty vision is failing."

Ned chuckled lightly as he put the transmission into reverse to turn around. Just then the car that had been tailing them pulled up directly behind the couple!

"Oh, no!" Nancy cried, as four teenage boys, all wearing jackets with sinister-looking spider patches on them, jumped out and swarmed around her car!

They grinned maliciously at the couple. Nancy and Ned hastily locked their doors and started to roll up their windows. One of the boys, however, was too quick for Nancy. He reached into the car before the pane was all the way up, shoved her hand aside, and pulled open the door, dragging Nancy out.

Ned, unable to prevent this, frantically pressed the horn, trying to attract the attention of anyone

near enough to hear him. Just then, another boy
pulled him away from behind the wheel and, with
the help of one of his friends, lifted him out of the
car.

Ned struggled furiously and quickly regained his
balance. He dived at the two boys, as another
young punk swung at him from behind.

"Ned, watch it!" Nancy cried. She stood next to
the boy who had dragged her out of the car. Apparently convinced she was too scared to move, he
left her unguarded and joined in the fray.

Ned, hearing her warning, ducked and, gripping
the legs of his attacker, pulled him to the ground.

Nancy knew she would be unable to assist Ned
in the fight. She turned and ran down the street as
fast as she could!

"Hey! Stop her!" one of the gang members
shouted. The boy who had dragged Nancy from
the car dashed after her. His long legs carried him
closer and closer to the fleeing girl, when Nancy
turned a corner. Her pursuer followed suit, but
suddenly he cried out in pain! He had stepped into
a pothole and fallen headlong onto the pavement.

Nancy looked over her shoulder and realized
that he was unable to get up. Relieved, she ran on,
calling loudly for help.

Ned, meanwhile, had been overpowered by the
three young hoodlums who remained behind.

Panting and exhausted, he stopped fighting. "What do you want?" he asked his attackers.

"We're going to take your car apart, wise guy!" one of the boys replied. He ran to the trunk of his own car and got out a box of tools. "Here," he said to one of his companions, "you disconnect the radio. I'll get the hubcaps."

The third boy, who was the smallest and looked about fifteen years old, stood guard over Ned.

While his friends were busily working on Nancy's car, he released his grip on the athlete somewhat. Ned, perfectly still, tried to regain his strength. Suddenly he twisted his body and grabbed the boy, lifting him up and dragging him toward the road barrier.

"Let me go!" the boy screeched, trying to get away from Ned.

The captive thrashed his legs, allowing his body to fall like dead weight toward the ground. But Ned tightened his grip on the boy's arms and, kicking over one of the wooden horses, he dragged him to the dark, swirling water.

"Tell your friends to quit or I'll dump you in the river!" he panted.

By now the boy's companions had come after Ned and his captive, ready to pounce on the young athlete again, when they heard police sirens in the distance.

"The cops!" one of the young punks yelled. "Let's get out of here!"

The two ran up the street, too scared to come to their friend's help.

"Just who are all of you?" Ned asked his captive.

"Friends!" the boy hissed, squirming and trying to kick Ned in the shins.

Ned sank his fingers into the boy's arm.

He bellowed in pain, but did not answer when Ned repeated the question.

"As soon as the police get here," Ned said, "I'm going to tell them you were responsible for this whole mess."

"But that's not true. Sammy Johnson made us do it," the boy blurted out.

"Who's he?"

After a slight hesitation, the answer came. "He's Matey Johnson's brother!"

By now, a patrol car flashing blue and red lights had pulled to a halt behind the two cars. Two officers and Nancy emerged. She rushed to Ned's side.

"Are you okay?" she inquired, noticing a slight bruise along his cheekbone.

Ned grinned. "I feel as though I just scored a touchdown—"

"I hate you," his captive snapped at Nancy.

She stared at him in surprise. "I don't even know you! What did I ever do to you?"

Before he could answer, the police officers interrupted. "Come on, we're taking you down to headquarters," one of the men said.

Immediately Ned related what the boy had told him. "I guess the kids were trying to get even with Nancy for catching Matey Johnson," he concluded.

"Incredible," the girl detective said. "Was Sammy one of the gang members?"

The boy, who was now handcuffed, glared. "Well, you won't catch him!"

Staring at her car stuck between the roadblock and the gang's vehicle, Nancy replied, "I guess I won't."

Before long, however, a tow truck was on the scene to move the boys' car. As soon as Nancy's hubcaps were replaced, the couple was ready to leave.

"Too bad the radio was ripped out," Ned said, looking at the hole, the wires dangling under the dashboard. "But at least they didn't take it with them. I'll have it put back for you while you're away."

"That's really nice of you," said the girl, adding, "I couldn't get over how you tackled all those kids. You were terrific."

Prompted to tell Nancy the full details of the final capture, he said, "I just dragged that little squirt to the goalpost—I mean the river!"

Ned turned the car around and drove toward the

49

main street once again, while Nancy looked at her watch.

"It's too late for us to go to the show," she said. "Why don't we go straight to the dance and meet everybody there? I'm sure Bess, George, and the boys are really worried about us."

Ned agreed. As Nancy had predicted, their friends were extremely anxious when they arrived.

"Where have you been?" George questioned, observing their disheveled attire. "Were you attacked by a monster?"

"Four of them," Nancy replied, urging Ned to tell the story.

When he had finished, George remarked, "Being captain of the football team sure comes in handy sometimes. But I never knew they trained you for multiple attacks."

Ned grinned. "We might not have fared so well if it hadn't been for our fleet-footed Nancy. Man, can she sprint!"

"But I'd rather dance!" Nancy laughed, as the orchestra music swelled in the hall. Ned took Nancy's hand and led her onto the dance floor. "Do your bones ache too much to dance?" she asked with concern.

"Never!" He laughed, sweeping the girl toward the center of the room.

The other two couples followed them. Bess,

however, was more perplexed than her cousin about Nancy's casual attitude.

"Look at them," she said, keeping her eyes on Nancy and Ned. "They're dancing and laughing as if nothing happened."

"Maybe," Dave chuckled, "Ned's feat did wonders for their relationship!"

As they found themselves dancing near Nancy and Ned, Bess said to her friend, "You ought to call your father and tell him you're all right. I phoned him, thinking possibly you went home for some reason."

Taking Bess's advice, Nancy excused herself for a few moments. Her father and Hannah Gruen were relieved to hear that she and Ned were safe after the attack.

"Those boys must be punished," Carson Drew declared. "The people in this town won't tolerate such nonsense." He paused, adding lightly, "Have a good time, dear, but stay together as a group on your way home." Nancy promised they would.

In the course of the evening, the young people discussed Nancy's manuscript and the mystery involving François Lefèvre's lace cuffs. "I'd also like to know who owns that diamond cross," Burt Eddleton spoke up. "You'll sure have plenty to keep you busy in Belgium."

"They'll be so busy, they won't even have the

time to send us postcards," Dave remarked.

The day the girls were to leave for New York, the boys drove them to the airport, stopping briefly at the post office on the way. To Nancy's amazement a copy of the signed receipt for the manuscript had just been received. But the signature was illegible. The young detective showed it to her friends, then put it in her purse.

"Besides that little gem," Ned said, "did you pack your toothbrush, your clothes, and a picture of me?"

"I did—in just the reverse order," she said, kissing Ned good-bye. "I'll bring you back a surprise!"

"Make it a solution to the secret in the old lace!"

When the threesome reached New York City, they took a taxi directly to Aunt Eloise Drew's apartment house. She welcomed the girls with hugs and kisses. After they were settled, Nancy told her aunt everything that had happened so far.

Aunt Eloise was shocked. "Terrible, just terrible!" she exclaimed. Then, looking fondly at her niece, she said, "I'm sorry to tell you this, Nancy, but the editor-in-chief of *Circle and Square* magazine wants to see you as soon as possible."

"Did he say why?" Nancy asked.

"Well, yes," Aunt Eloise replied, unsure of what to say next. She took a deep breath.

"I can take it," Nancy insisted.

"It seems there's a serious charge against you!"

# 7

## *The Stolen Bag*

"What kind of charge?" George asked. "Nancy hasn't done anything wrong."

Aunt Eloise put an arm around her niece. "Of course she hasn't. My brother phoned me a little while ago with the message. He said Mr. Miller, the man to whom I gave your manuscript, didn't give any details, but he stressed he must see you personally."

"It's almost five-thirty," Nancy said. "The magazine office is probably closed now. I'll have to go there first thing in the morning."

The following day, she set up an appointment to see Mr. Miller.

"I'm going with you," Bess insisted. "After

what's happened to you, I don't think you should travel *anywhere* alone."

"Bess is right," George agreed. "I'll come along too."

Nancy's face creased into a broad smile. "With two bodyguards to protect me, I guess I ought to be fairly safe."

"And if all else fails," her plump friend teased her, "we'll call Ned to the rescue!"

Aunt Eloise, who taught school, had already left so the visitors tidied the apartment before leaving for the office of *Circle and Square* magazine.

Once outside, the girls headed west past a small private park toward Madison Avenue, one of New York City's busiest streets. It was filled with taxis, passenger cars, and crowds of pedestrians walking at a faster clip than any vehicle could move that morning.

"I just love New York," Bess swooned, gazing into the window of an Italian dress boutique. "The clothes are gorgeous, the people are gorgeous—" She paused to stare at a sleek, black-haired girl in the shop. She was wearing a fine lemon-colored knit suit. "Boy, I wish I could look like that."

George nudged her cousin away from the window. "You could if you stopped eating!"

Bess pretended not to hear the remark. "Nancy, wouldn't it be great to see a few shows and concerts too?"

"I hardly have enough time to see Mr. Miller," Nancy said, her thoughts miles away from Madison Avenue. "But maybe we can catch up with New York when we return."

Soon the trio reached the entrance of a tall building where they found a wall directory next to a bank of elevators. *Circle and Square* magazine was on the twelfth floor.

As they rode up in silence, Nancy steadied her eyes on the floor indicator. When the light stopped at twelve, the doors slid open slowly and she took a deep breath.

George leaned toward her. "Don't worry," she said, as they entered the magazine office. "Everything will turn out all right."

Mr. Miller proved to be a handsome man with light brown hair and cheerful blue eyes. Nancy judged him to be close to her father's age.

"I have an eighteen-year-old daughter too," he volunteered. "She looks a little bit like you, Miss Drew, but I'm afraid the resemblance ends there. She would never plagiarize someone's story."

The accusation stunned the girl detective. "Well, I wouldn't either," she replied evenly, trying to check her rising temper.

"That's right," Bess said in support.

"Why don't you let Mr. Miller explain what he means," George suggested.

The editor-in-chief said that his readers had

found two identical entries to the contest. "One of them is yours," he stated. "Your solution to the mystery is the same as the other contestant's."

"Word for word?" Nancy inquired.

"Well, no," he replied, "but it certainly looks like a clear-cut case of plagiarism or mental telepathy. Which is it?"

The girl detective gritted her teeth as she proceeded to answer. She told about Matey Johnson and his attempted break-in.

"But now you say he's in jail," Mr. Miller replied. "Did he manage to steal your manuscript?"

"No," Nancy admitted, suddenly realizing Johnson had had no opportunity to see her entry. "But he overheard me talking about it! Then I mailed you my original, which your office claims never arrived. Yet I have a receipt that says otherwise. Then my aunt delivered a copy of my story several days ago."

Nancy opened her purse and took out the receipt with the illegible signature on it.

"Strange, very strange," Mr. Miller said, frowning. "This doesn't look familiar to me. I'm sure it didn't come from here."

"What?" George cried. "But the receipt was returned to Nancy by the River Heights post office!"

"You'll have to leave it with me," Mr. Miller said abruptly. "This is most irregular."

Worried that she might lose an important clue to

56

the identity of the plagiarist, Nancy asked for a photocopy of the tiny paper.

"Don't you trust me?" the editor quipped, showing the first sign of friendliness.

Ignoring the comment, Nancy said, "Can you figure out the signature? We can't."

"No, but I'm inclined to think it belongs to someone who doesn't work in this office."

"Possibly my rival in the contest," the girl sleuth concluded. "Who is it, by the way?"

"A man named Paul Frieden." As Mr. Miller stared at the illegible signature, he added, somewhat embarrassed, "I may owe you an apology for my attitude when you walked in here this morning. But I'm afraid that until this matter is resolved, we cannot enter either your manuscript or Mr. Frieden's in our contest."

"Oh, that's awful!" Bess burst out in Nancy's defense. "She wrote every word of the story herself. She didn't steal anything from anybody!"

"I admire your loyalty," Mr. Miller remarked, "but rules are—"

"Nancy's an amateur detective," George interrupted, "so naturally that's why she was able to make up such an interesting ending to the story of François Lefèvre."

"I'm sure—" Mr. Miller started again, but George would not let him finish.

"Nancy hoped to win first prize and give the

money to a very worthy charity," she said pleadingly.

Mr. Miller led the disappointed visitors to the door. "I'm truly sorry about this whole thing. Look, here's what I'll do. I'll request my staff to hold both manuscripts until the very last minute of the deadline, which has been extended a bit. Perhaps we'll know by then what really happened."

Nancy smiled faintly. "Thank you very much."

"That's the best I can do," the man said, shaking her hand.

Hopeful that Mr. Drew might be able to work on Nancy's case while they were away, the girls left New York on a night flight to Brussels, Belgium. From there they planned to take a train or drive to Brugge, since the small city had no airport of its own.

As the plane's wheels touched down, George stared out the window at the sun-soaked terminal building. It was noon in Belgium which meant it was only 6:00 A.M. in New York.

The travelers passed through Immigration and Passport Control quickly, then headed for the baggage area. One by one, pieces of luggage appeared on the moving conveyor. First George, then Bess saw their suitcases and pulled them off. Nancy also spotted hers, a sturdy green bag, but waited for it to come closer before taking it. Suddenly, to her astonishment, a man at the head of the line reached out, grabbed the bag, and hurried away.

"Did you see that?" Nancy cried out. "A man stole my suitcase!" She dashed through the crowd of passengers. A guard stopped her abruptly at a doorway leading to the exit. She could not pass through until her luggage was cleared by a customs official.

"But someone just took my bag!" she exclaimed indignantly. "He went through this door!"

"Well, evidently he works here and has proper identification. Maybe the bag just looks like yours."

Nancy rejoined Bess and George, hopeful that another green bag bearing her initials would appear. None did. Completely frustrated, Nancy spoke to the guard again, insisting she had seen someone take her luggage.

"If so," the guard replied, "I suggest you report it to our lost and found office. Most likely, the person will return it when he realizes he has the wrong bag. Come back tomorrow morning and check."

Following the man's instructions, Nancy and her friends went to the lost and found desk and reported the theft. Afterward they decided to stay in Brussels overnight.

"Oh, well," Bess said, "look at the bright side. This is where François lived!"

She and George tagged after Nancy to a shuttle

train which was headed for the heart of the city. They chose a quaint hotel listed in Nancy's pocket directory that was within walking distance of the station.

"Belgium is a three-language country," Bess said. "People speak either French, Dutch, or Flemish depending on where they live. Many, of course, speak all three."

Despite the beauty of the city and her friends' attempts to cheer her, Nancy's thoughts were solely on the missing luggage.

Somebody wants to keep me from going to Brugge! she thought as she crept into bed that night. But who?

# 8

## Detective Trouble

Nancy slept fitfully and awoke early the next morning. She showered and dressed before her traveling companions had awakened, then went for a short walk until George and Bess were ready for breakfast. In the dining room, the girls discussed their situation.

"I have a hunch that someone is trying to stall our visit to Brugge," Nancy said, sampling one of the sweet rolls on her plate.

Bess gulped down a cup of tea. "Can't," she said.

"What do you mean 'can't'?" George questioned.

"If Nancy's bag doesn't show up today," her cousin replied, "we'll go on to Brugge and tell the airline to forward it to Madame Chambray's."

To Nancy's disappointment, the green suitcase had not been returned to the airport. She gave the address she would be staying at in Brugge and begged the airline representative to deliver the luggage as soon as it arrived.

"Frankly," Nancy said to her friends, "I doubt it will ever come. I'm positive that the person who took my bag did so on purpose."

Noticing a policeman standing outside the main entrance to the terminal, Nancy walked up to him.

"*Monsieur,*" she called. "Do you speak English?"

"*Un peu*—a little."

The girl detective explained that her suitcase had probably been stolen.

"Can you describe the man—slowly, please?"

Nancy said he had been too far away for her to give a thorough description. "But I can tell you this. He was tall and thin and wore a dark blue suit or uniform. When I reported him to the guard, he said the person probably worked here."

The officer paused a moment before speaking again. "Can you point the guard out to me so I can question him?"

The girl ducked back into the terminal, glancing in the direction of the baggage area. A different man was on duty there. When she returned to re-

port this, she added one more identifying clue—
the initials *ND* on her suitcase.

"Perhaps all your trouble is simply based on coincidence," the officer said. "The man who took
your bag may, in fact, own one just like yours."

"And his name begins with the same letters as
mine?" The young sleuth completed the policeman's deduction. "That would certainly be a coincidence."

"Well, I will file a report for you and maybe
your suitcase will be found."

"If so, could you forward it to Brugge? We'll be
going there today." She gave the officer Madame
Chambray's address and thanked him for his help.
Then the girls took the shuttle train to the railroad
station.

The ride to Brugge was uneventful. The girls
watched the flat, green landscape and talked little.
Finally, after a stop in Ghent, they reached the
medieval town of Brugge. It was quaintly pictur-
esque with lots of narrow streets and three- or
four-story old stone houses often separated by canals.

"This is like traveling back into history to the
Middle Ages," Bess remarked.

Her cousin was intrigued by the canal boats.
Several of them were open motorboats while others were canopied with colorful awnings. "No won-

der Brugge is called the Venice of the North."

Rather than take a land taxi, the visitors chose a boat. The *schipper,* a man whose ruddy complexion indicated he spent many hours at the wheel, stowed their luggage and started the motor.

It chugged loudly, causing Bess to whisper, "Maybe this is a medieval motor!"

Nancy smiled halfheartedly. "I hope the dress shops aren't," she said, wishing she had worn her new sweater-coat on the plane. She wondered if she would ever see it again.

As the *schipper* steered the boat from one canal into another, it passed under a small stone bridge with a Gothic hump in the middle. Beyond was a fieldstone house evidently built centuries ago. The narrow back windows were set under arches beneath a triangular roof.

"That must be where Madame Chambray lives," George announced, as the boatman tied the craft to a post.

He helped the girls out, and unloaded the larger pieces of luggage. Then he grabbed the smaller ones, including Bess's cosmetic bag. She held her hand out to take it, but the bag slipped through the man's fingers, splashing into the water.

"Oh, no!" Bess cried out. "There go all my lipsticks and nail polish!"

The *schipper* jabbered something unintelligible.

Nancy caught the word *droevig,* which she figured probably meant "sorry."

"Do be careful!" Bess pleaded while the man hopped back into the boat and picked up a pole with a grappling hook at one end. He slid it into the water and fished slowly for the handle of the case. In a few moments he nodded happily. He had caught the little bag!

"Thank goodness," Bess sighed.

"You and your makeup," her cousin needled her. "Why wear rouge at all when you know I can keep your blood pressure sky-high!"

By now, the boatman had picked up their luggage and was leading the way to the door of the house. It opened, revealing a tall, slender woman with silver-gray hair wound into a knot at the nape of her neck.

"Madame Chambray?" Nancy inquired.

"*Mais oui,*" she said in French. "Yes, and welcome."

The girls introduced themselves, and Nancy paid the *schipper.* Once they were seated in the living room, the visitors were struck by its charm. It contained numerous pieces of intricately carved furniture and heavy brocade draperies. Many of the paintings on the walls had been done by very fine artists, some of them famous.

Nancy was eager to see the diamond and lapis lazuli cross but decided to wait for Madame Chambray to mention it first.

"I am so glad you could come," the woman said. "You know I've been living in this house only a very short while but already it has produced—how you say—a mystery?"

"Yes, you wrote to Mother about it," Bess said.

"Then you understand I am looking for the owner of a beautiful cross," Madame Chambray continued.

Nancy felt obligated to warn her not to tell her story to too many people.

"No?" the woman replied, raising her eyebrows. "But how will I ever find the owner? I must tell you I put an article in the newspaper about it. Let me show it to you." The well-meaning woman excused herself for a moment and returned with a news clipping which she handed to Nancy.

Immediately the girl detective's eyes fell on her own name. "You mentioned my visit here as well," Nancy said in disbelief.

"It isn't every day that a famous young detective comes to Brugge." The woman chuckled.

"Oh, dear," Bess moaned. "All your chances of working under cover, Nancy, just vanished into thin air!"

Madame Chambray caught the look of disappointment on Nancy's face. "Is there a problem?"

she asked. "Did I do something wrong?"

George replied first. "No, but—"

"But what?" Madame Chambray said anxiously.

"Nancy may not be able to solve your mystery," Bess declared boldly.

# 9

## The Ghost

Nancy was less pessimistic than her friends and smiled at Madame Chambray. "Let's just say you've given me—all of us—quite a challenge," she said. "The more people who know about the diamond cross and your search for its owner, the more chance there is that someone will put in a false claim."

The woman chided herself. "How stupid I am!" she exclaimed. "That never occurred to me."

It was obvious to her visitors that Madame Chambray was scrupulously honest and very trusting. No doubt she could be easily swayed by the sympathetic tale of a con artist.

"Where did you find the cross?" Nancy inquired. She gazed toward the narrow hallway where steps led to the second and third stories and tried to imagine how Madame Chambray had stumbled upon the glittering piece in some medieval nook upstairs.

"It was in a most unlikely place," the woman said, pausing. "In the cellar."

"The cellar?" George repeated in surprise. "Was it in a box or just lying on the floor somewhere?"

"Actually it was wrapped in a piece of linen that was caught in the stonework—"

Madame Chambray stopped speaking for a moment and went into another room. When she returned, she held a small purple velvet box in her hand. "You must see it—it is so beautiful," she said, giving the box to Nancy to open.

Bess and George gathered near the young detective as she lifted the cover. Inside lay the dazzling cross.

"It's exquisite!" Bess exclaimed while Nancy removed the piece from the box to examine it closely.

The oblong diamonds and lapis lazuli stones were set in solid gold. But there were no unusual markings on the setting.

"The linen I found it wrapped in," Madame Chambray said, "is folded under the mount in the box."

George took the cross from Nancy, enabling her to remove the linen. "There's something stitched on it," Nancy commented as she stared at the line of French words embroidered on the soiled material. Below them was the name *Antoinette Tissot*.

"Maybe the cross belonged to King Louis XVI," Bess suggested with a grin.

Madame Chambray interrupted the conversation, asking Nancy if she could interpret the message.

"I think so," the girl detective replied. "Doesn't it say, 'God protect you wherever you go'?"

"That's correct," the woman said with admiration.

"Have you shown this to anyone else?" Nancy questioned.

"Other than some friends, I did ask an expert appraiser of antique jewelry to look at the cross. He estimates it to be more than one hundred years old."

"Which means," George said, "Antoinette is not living anymore."

"Possibly," Nancy put in, "but not necessarily. After all, the cross could have come into her possession years after it was made." She stifled a yawn, suddenly feeling extremely tired after their adventure in Brussels.

"I can see you are a very smart detective, Nancy," said Madame Chambray, "but I don't want you to trouble your mind about all of this right now. You need your sleep. You all do."

She took the little velvet box from the girls and replaced the linen and beautiful cross.

"I am having a small dinner party this evening to introduce you to my friends. They are so eager to meet all of you," the woman went on. "So—"

"But I have nothing appropriate to wear," Nancy murmured worriedly. She told Madame Chambray about her missing luggage, adding, "Is there a dress shop nearby?"

"There are plenty of shops," Madame Chambray replied. "But you must rest. I will find something for you to wear. Don't worry."

Madame Chambray led the girls upstairs to their rooms, each one charmingly decorated with silk-covered beds and matching drapes. George lent Nancy a robe which she changed into before collapsing on her pillow.

The girl detective's mind whirled endlessly about the new, exciting mystery. To whom did the antique cross belong? Someone—apparently Antoinette—had given it to someone else, but when and why? There were few clues to go on, fewer than those about the secret in the old lace.

When Nancy awoke, she felt a surge of energy.

We ought to investigate the cellar, she decided,

quickly getting out of bed. Maybe we'll find an important lead down there.

Except for the sound of an approaching motorboat, the house was very quiet. Nancy pressed her nose against the casement window. She noticed Madame Chambray at the dock, waiting to board the boat. Maybe she's going shopping for the party tonight, the girl thought, then went to the room next door.

"Wake up, Bess!" she called. "We have work to do!"

Her friend was sleeping peacefully, oblivious to Nancy, who was jostling her now. "Wha-what is it?" Bess finally mumbled.

"Come on, lazybones, get up. We're going on a hunt for clues!"

Next Nancy knocked on George's door, then went back to her own room where she put on her skirt and sweater. The young detectives, their flashlights in hand, gathered in the corridor at the top of the steps.

"Where do we start?" Bess asked.

"In the cellar," Nancy said, "since that's where Madame Chambray found the cross."

The girls noticed a heavy wooden door off the kitchen. It creaked noisily as Nancy swung it back on its hinges and saw that it led below. Before descending, Nancy thought she heard something underneath the stairwell but dismissed it when the noise was not repeated. Step by step she guided her friends into the eerie darkness.

"I'm scared." Bess shivered. "Nancy, why don't we wait for Madame Chambray to return before we go any farther?"

"Sh!" George quieted her cousin. "Stop pretending to be a chicken detective."

"Who's pretending?" Bess laughed nervously.

As they stood in the musty, dark room, they beamed their lights on the stone walls, looking unsuccessfully for a switch to turn on an overhead light.

"Oh!" Bess cried out suddenly while Nancy and George walked ahead of her.

"What's the matter?" Nancy asked.

"I hear weird noises. Don't you?"

"No," the other detectives whispered back.

"Stick closer," George said, but her cousin continued to lag behind.

Nancy swept her flashlight across a deep stony crevice in one wall while George examined the floor beneath it. "Swing your light over here, Bess," George requested, unaware that her cousin was not with them. But when no response came, George spun around. "Bess, where are you?"

Instantly Nancy flashed her light toward the cellar steps where they had started their investigation. Bess was nowhere in sight. A couple of tense minutes later, they saw a ghostly figure in white standing beyond the fringe of light!

Nancy turned her flashlight on the mysterious apparition, noticing it wore leather boots. "Who are you?" she cried out.

There was no answer.

"Let's get him, George!" Nancy hissed, feeling the two girls had a good chance to overpower the lone ghost, who seemed to be a tall, slender man.

"Right!" George said, and both charged toward the figure, diving for the sheet that covered him. The ghost threw out his arms and with a powerful thrust flung both girls to the floor. Their lights fell out of their hands and went out. Now they were in total darkness.

George screamed, expecting the ghost to pounce on them at any moment. All they heard, however, were a few shuffling noises that quickly faded.

A bit shaken, the young detectives groped for their flashlights. George found hers first and beamed it toward Nancy, who had noticed a small hole right next to where she had fallen. "I—I think my light rolled in there," she said.

"Where's the ghost?" George asked, now beaming her light in the direction where the apparition had stood. All she could see was the cellar wall.

The ghost had vanished. Was he hiding nearby

ready to attack them again? And where was Bess?

Had he kidnapped her?

Panic-stricken, both girls shrieked, calling out, "Bess! Bess!"

# 10

## *The Water Tunnel*

Nancy and George called Bess's name several times but there was no response. "What could have happened to her?" George asked in bewilderment.

Then they heard a muffled sound. Keeping quiet, Nancy took George's flashlight and edged toward the cellar steps. There, under the staircase, was a door made of heavy wood and painted the color of the stonework.

"George, help me!" Nancy said, tugging on the iron bolt. Her fingers, wet with perspiration, slipped.

George grasped the bolt firmly and yanked it back. The door swung open, revealing a small closet. Inside was Bess, a gag stuffed across her mouth, her wrists and ankles bound tightly. She sat on the floor, leaning against the cold stone wall, where spiders had fastened their cobwebs.

"Oh, Bess!" Nancy gasped.

"Are you all right?" George cried, quickly bending over her cousin to remove the gag from her mouth.

"Who did this to you?" Nancy asked as she went to work on the ropes that were tied around the girl's wrists and legs.

"A—a man!" Bess murmured. "He was dressed like a ghost. Oh, it was horrible!"

"Poor Bess," George said sympathetically, massaging the red welts where the rope had cut into her cousin's wrists.

"He—he came out of that closet," Bess went on. "He grabbed my flashlight, then put the gag over my mouth."

"Did he say anything to you?" Nancy asked.

"No, nothing."

"We must report this to the police," George said resolutely as Bess slowly stumbled to her feet.

Despite the ache in her ankles, the girl insisted on climbing the stairs without help. "I don't want to stay down here one more second."

When they emerged into the kitchen, the girls heard the back door open and close.

"That must be Madame Chambray," Nancy said, calling out her name.

"Yes, dear, I'm home," the woman replied, joining her young guests. Madame Chambray's smile quickly changed to a deep frown when she saw the smudges on Bess's face and the stains on her skirt. "Did you fall?"

Tears welled up in the girl's eyes as she said no and explained what had happened.

"*Ma pauvre chérie*," the woman said, hugging Bess briefly. She rinsed a small towel in lukewarm water and patted the girl's face. "There, there, you will be fine again."

"Oh, thank you," Bess said. "I do feel better."

"How did this terrible man get into my house?" Madame Chambray asked. "Maybe we should call the police."

"Well, he's gone now," Nancy said, adding, "Is there some sort of connection between the basement and the canal?"

"Not that I know of. I haven't lived here very long and I am still learning about the house. It seems to be full of little doors and nooks and crannies so there may well be an underground passage."

That was all the young detectives needed to hear. "Are you game to go back down?" Nancy asked George, knowing that Bess was not up to it.

"Why not?"

"Please don't," Bess pleaded. "The ghost may try to stick you both in that awful closet!"

"We'll be careful," Nancy promised. "And we'll send up a report every ten minutes. Okay?"

As she and George hurried below, Bess asked to be excused.

"By all means," Madame Chambray said. "Take a good hot bath and relax. You want to look your prettiest tonight!"

She winked at the girl, causing Bess to wonder if she was planning to introduce her guests to some charming young Belgian men. "Oh, I will!" Bess giggled, leaving her hostess alone in the kitchen.

Madame Chambray busied herself with some last-minute dinner preparations. Then, glancing at the package she had brought home for Nancy, the woman smiled happily.

I think she will like it, Madame Chambray thought. I'll put it on her bed, so when she comes up she'll find a nice surprise.

She stepped out into the hallway and was about to go upstairs when she spied someone staring through the living room window.

"Who's there?" she called out.

The figure ducked quickly out of sight, prompting Madame Chambray to drop the package and run to the door. She opened it and stuck her head outside.

"Is anyone there?" she repeated.

But the only response was the water of the canals gently lapping against the walls of the house.

How strange! she said to herself.

Nancy and George, in the meantime, were exploring one end of the cellar where they discovered another door. It opened onto a short tunnel of water.

"I'm sure this is how the ghost got in," Nancy remarked. "I wonder how deep the water is. Maybe he waded in and out."

"Did his boots look wet to you?" George questioned.

"I couldn't tell—they looked dark to begin with."

"I'll go upstairs and get a yardstick," George volunteered. "That way we can find out how deep it is." She rushed off.

Nancy, however, became impatient and went down to the lowest step. Maybe I can tell by sticking my hand in, she thought.

She kneeled down, lowering her arm into the water. Her fingers did not touch bottom. Guess I'll have to stretch out, she decided.

The stone step shifted slightly as she lay flat, then slipped forward ready to sink into the murky pool!

Oh, no! Nancy panicked, trying to hold her position until George returned. "George!" she cried loudly. "Help me!"

George could not hear her friend from upstairs where Madame Chambray was telling her about the stranger at the window.

Oh, why doesn't she come? Nancy thought in alarm as she tried to grab the dry step above her, praying it would not also give way.

Fortunately, George had not lingered too long in conversation with Madame Chambray and was on her way back downstairs. She raced to the tunnel door, shouting to Nancy, "Wait until you hear what—" and then broke off when she saw Nancy's predicament.

George dropped the yardstick on the top step and gripped Nancy's arm, helping her up, as the stone step crumbled into the water.

"Where would I be without you, friend?" Nancy said gratefully.

"Swimming," George quipped.

Nancy laughed as the other girl lowered the yardstick into the water. It was shallower than she had estimated. When George pulled the stick out, it was covered with weeds and muck up to a foot and a half.

"That man could have waded out of here very easily," Nancy concluded. "And a boat could have been waiting for him out on the canal. Of course, the big question is why— Why did he come here at all?"

Had he planned to burglarize Madame Chambray's house while she was out? Was he pursuing the diamond cross or something even more precious? The girl detectives tried to piece the puzzle together.

"But what could be more valuable than the cross?" George said to her friend. "Of course, the furnishings and paintings must be worth a lot—"

Nancy snapped her fingers. "Didn't Madame Chambray mention in her letter to Mrs. Marvin something about a document and—and a treasure?"

"Yes, you're right. I completely forgot about that."

"I almost did too."

"But how would the ghost know the contents of the letter?" George asked.

"He wouldn't unless he's André Bergère," Nancy said grimly.

"Not necessarily," George said after thinking for a moment. "Since Madame Chambray talked so openly with her friends about these things, they may have inadvertently passed the information along to another would-be thief!"

Nancy was eager to ask their hostess about the mysterious treasure and stepped toward the tunnel door. The chugging sound of a motorboat stopped her midway.

"Look!" she cried, pointing toward the canal.

The boat was entering the tunnel. Who was steering it? Had their ghostly attacker returned?

# 11

## Fantastic News

The oncoming boat drew closer. George clicked off her flashlight, waiting for the single occupant to reach the steps.

"When he gets here," Nancy whispered, "shine your light right in his face. We'll be able to capture him then!"

The boat, however, stopped some distance away. A man who was carrying a large bundle hopped out and entered another door at the base of the tunnel.

"I guess he lives next door," Nancy remarked with a giggle.

George also laughed in relief. "I'm glad he wasn't our ghost after all," she said and seized the chance to relate Madame Chambray's story about the stranger at the window.

"I wonder if he and Mr. Ghost are one and the same," Nancy commented, leading the way back to the kitchen. "We have so much to talk about with Madame Chambray." She glanced at her watch. "But it's nearly dinnertime."

Upstairs the girls found the woman peering into a large kettle on the stove. The aroma of delicate spices filled the air.

"What are you making?" Nancy said. "It smells absolutely delicious."

"*Waterzooi*." The woman smiled. "One of our traditional dishes—poached capon in a light creamy sauce. The rest of the menu is a surprise. And so is the package on your bed, Nancy. Now go up to your room and get ready. My guests will be arriving soon."

Excitedly the girl dashed upstairs and opened the bundle. Folded carefully inside was a beautiful ecru linen dress trimmed in fine lace!

"Oh, it's lovely!" the girl detective exclaimed happily.

She held up the dress in front of her and gazed into the full-length mirror in the corner of the room. Around the neckline and fitted cuffs of the long, tight sleeves were ruffles of lace. I wonder if François Lefèvre's lace cuffs were like these, Nancy said to herself. Then, hearing Madame Chambray come up the stairs, the girl hurried out of her room. "Oh, thank you so much, Madame—"

Embarrassed, the woman cut her off, telling her to dress quickly. "Everyone will be here in a few minutes!" she said with a smile.

To her delight, the three girls were ready to greet the guests when they arrived. Madame Chambray introduced Professor Philip Permeke and his daughter Hilda, a pretty blond who looked about twenty. With her was a young man with sturdy features and brooding green eyes.

He's cute, Bess thought, but he looks so sad. I wonder why.

"And this is Joseph Stolk," Madame Chambray announced as Bess shook his hand. "He and Hilda went to high school together. Now Joseph is studying art history in Brussels."

"Oh, how interesting!" Bess said eagerly. "I bet you know a lot about all the museums of this wonderful old town. Perhaps you could take us on a tour sometime." She flashed him a dazzling, flirtatious smile.

"Yes—uh—perhaps I could," Joseph replied shyly.

Hilda seemed less than delighted with that suggestion, and George tugged on her cousin's arm, signaling her not to pursue the conversation any farther. "You're about to set off a little quarrel between those two," she whispered to Bess. Then, turning to the professor, she said, "Dr. Permeke, I understand that you are an expert on the history of Brugge. Would you tell us a little about it?"

"Gladly," he said, "but stop me when you get bored."

His remarks during dinner were fascinating. "Did you know that the original town of Brugge was on the seacoast? The name of our ancient town means city of bridges. Long ago it was a thriving port. But storms were so devastating, even the dikes could not save it. The merchants moved inland—to the spot where we are today—and dug a canal to connect the town with the ocean."

"That was quite an engineering feat," Madame Chambray commented. "It's about ten miles from here to the coast."

The jovial gray-haired professor nodded. "When this new town was built, its predecessor on the coast took the name of Zeebrugge which means Sea Brugge."

While he paused to take a sip of wine, his daughter continued the tale. "This was a very fashionable place in the fifteenth, sixteenth, and seventeenth centuries. Merchants were rather successful and able to buy the finest of everything, including the best clothes from Paris. If you like, I'll give you a tour tomorrow."

"Perhaps I can go with you too," Joseph suggested, looking over at Bess for a moment.

Hilda's suspicious glance trailed from him to Bess, who was beaming prettily. "I think not," Hilda said firmly. "Don't you have a term paper to finish before the end of the week?"

"Yes, but I—"

Poor Joseph is trapped under Hilda's jealous thumb! Bess decided.

Seeing the fire grow in the young Belgian woman's face, George quickly changed the subject. "Maybe Hilda can take us to a gift shop where I can buy something for Burt and you can buy something for Dave and—"

"I can buy something for Ned," Nancy chimed in.

"Are they your brothers?" Hilda inquired with interest. "Or, as you say in America, your boyfriends?"

Nancy grinned. "They're our boyfriends," she said, happy to see a smile return to Hilda's face.

"In that case," their new friend went on, "you must buy them very special gifts—and, of course, you will want some lace for yourselves."

The mention of lace prompted Nancy to reveal one of her reasons for coming to Brugge. She mentioned the magazine contest and the story of François Lefèvre."

"What?" Madame Chambray said, electrified. "What was that name you mentioned?"

"François Lefèvre."

The woman stared at her, unable to speak for a moment.

"What is it, Madame Chambray?" Nancy asked anxiously. "Is that name familiar to you?"

"*Mais oui*—yes, indeed," the woman cried out. "It is one of the names mentioned in the document I found. It was written by one Friedrich Vonderlicht, also known as François Lefèvre!"

"I don't believe it!" George blurted out. "You mean, François once owned this house?"

"Apparently he did!"

"Then maybe the secret in the old lace is hidden right under this roof!" Nancy deduced.

"I doubt it," Madame Chambray remarked. "After all, François lived here a long time ago. Others have come and gone since and I'm sure that whatever secrets he had were discovered by later occupants."

"Could we see the document, please?" Nancy urged.

"I locked it in my desk upstairs," Madame Chambray said. "I've been looking for my keys but can't seem to find them."

"Oh!" Bess said anxiously. "Do you think they were stolen?"

"No, dear." The woman smiled. "I always misplace them. I'm sure they're in the house somewhere and I'll find them tomorrow. No one would have any reason to steal them, so don't worry."

"But what does the document say?"

"It was a small part of a will, actually. It said that Friedrich Vonderlicht, also known as François Lefèvre, was leaving his fortune to his wife. But the part telling where he left it has been torn off."

"Too bad," George said. "I'm afraid it won't help us much then."

"Well, it's helped already," Bess pointed out. "Now we know that François lived in this house!"

The group discussed the strange coincidence at length, and the rest of the evening proved enjoyable as everyone moved into the living room to taste Madame Chambray's surprise dessert, a delectable lemon meringue pie.

"I'm stuffed," Bess admitted at last.

"Well, tomorrow we will walk off all the calories!" Hilda chuckled.

But before the visitors were ready to leave Madame Chambray's house the next morning, there was an impatient knock at the door.

"Will you answer it for me, please?" Madame Chambray asked Nancy. "I want to keep an eye on the toast."

The girl hurried out of the kitchen to the hallway and flung open the door. To her surprise, it was a *schipper* holding a piece of green luggage in his hand.

"That's my suitcase!" Nancy cried gleefully.

# 12

## At the Lace Center

"Where did you find my suitcase?" Nancy asked the boatman.

But he spoke no English. He merely smiled and waved good-bye, leaving the girl dumbstruck. Immediately Nancy looked through her bag to see if anything was missing. Nothing appeared to have been stolen. She told the good news to everyone before changing from the travel clothes she had worn since leaving New York, then called the airline for details.

"Someone found your bag in an alley behind a hotel in Brussels," a clerk told her. "Although your luggage tag was taken off, the airline tag wasn't. And we knew your initials, which helped us identify it."

Nancy repeated the conversation to her friends. "Now I'm totally convinced someone took it, hoping to keep me from leaving Brussels," she said. "Whoever it was is probably in Brugge this very minute."

When the threesome met Hilda, they asked her to take them to a lace shop. "I'd like to learn as much about lace making as possible," Nancy said.

"Then I know just where to go," the young Belgian woman said.

She led the girls to the Lace Center where supplies were sold and lace makers could take courses in their craft. There were two types of lace, Hilda explained: bobbin lace which originated in Belgium and needlepoint lace which developed at the same time in France.

"Those are bobbins," Hilda said, pointing to a tray of wooden objects which resembled miniature bowling pins. "They are attached to linen threads and serve as weights when the threads are combined in intricate patterns. But first, the *kantwerker* or lace maker chooses a wooden mold to work on. Like one of these."

She indicated a stack of disks about a foot and a half in diameter. One side of each disk was a mound covered with canvas. "They're called pillows and are filled with seaweed," the girl continued. "After the *kantwerker* chooses her pattern, she copies it with pins which she sticks into the pillow. The threads are woven around the pins and then the pins are pulled out."

George noticed sheets of transparent plastic. "What are these for?" she asked.

"The lace maker covers her pillow and the finished lace with a piece of plastic, leaving open just enough space for her to work on. The plastic helps keep the lace clean."

Nancy and Bess discovered a bin of linen threads. "Hannah would love these," Nancy said. While she purchased three spools, George wandered toward the rear of the shop. A chubby boy about eight years old was dipping his hands into another barrel. He pulled out a bunch of bobbins, and threw one at the window and the other at a small statue on a shelf.

"Stop it!" George exclaimed, rushing toward the boy and grabbing his arm.

"Says who?" he answered stubbornly.

"I do," George said, quietly challenging the boy.

He yanked away from her. As she dived for him again, he threw a bobbin at her, hitting her neck hard. Furious, George gripped him by the shoulders and shook him.

"Mommy! Mommy!" the boy yelled frantically.

"What's going on?" A woman suddenly appeared out of the crowd milling about the Lace Center.

"Your son just threw that at me!" George defended herself, pointing to the bobbin lying on the floor.

"Did you do that, Peter?" the boy's mother asked, grabbing the child's hand. The small boy started to protest but at his mother's stern look, lowered his head guiltily.

Meanwhile Nancy and Bess dashed toward their friend. "What happened?" Bess asked, noting the red spot on her cousin's neck.

"Lets just say I hope the next time I get this close to a bobbin I'll be making lace with it," George replied dryly.

"I apologize," the boy's mother said softly. "My husband and I have been dragging Peter with us everywhere and he's getting very cranky, though that's no excuse. I think we'll take him back to the hotel now." Still holding the little boy's hand she exited quickly.

Meanwhile, Nancy asked the shop owner if she had any ice on hand. The woman flew toward a back room and returned with a small bowl and cloth.

"This should prevent any swelling," Nancy said, wrapping the ice in the cloth.

George held the compress against her neck, insisting her friends continue their tour of the store. In a back room about twenty women were making lace. Their nimble fingers moved the bobbins with dizzying speed.

Nancy spoke to one of the lace makers who was seated in one corner, studying a book about lace.

"Could you tell us a few facts about your craft?" the girl detective asked.

"*Oui*. I'll try," she said, speaking slowly with a soft accent. "In the sixteenth and seventeenth centuries, lace was worth much money. It was very valuable as trim for clothing. Many people sold their homes and other belongings just to buy it."

"That's incredible," Nancy commented.

"Incredible but true. There are old papers that say Charles I of England bought forty-four yards of lace trim for a dozen collars and a dozen cuffs, and six hundred yards of bobbin lace for just his nightwear!"

The girls giggled. "Can you picture Dave or Ned wearing ruffled shirts and pajamas?" Bess said, as the woman handed her book to Nancy.

There were numerous photographs of lace patterns throughout. Birds and flowers predominated but there were geometric designs as well.

"Judging from these," Nancy said, "it wouldn't have been too difficult to hide a message in a pair of lace cuffs. It could have been easily woven among flowers and leaves or fantastic-looking birds, like this one." She pointed in the book to a picture of a bird with a striking fantail.

Bess agreed. "I can just imagine a young woman spending endless hours weaving a message for François like 'I must meet you soon in the garden of my home.' Or, 'A moonlit night would be best.' "

The girl's reverie was quickly interrupted, however, by her cousin and Hilda, who had been chatting with George. "My neck's a hundred percent better and we're ready to move on; are you?"

"If you say so," Nancy replied. "Where to, Hilda?"

"Well you did mention you'd like to go to the museums so I suggest the *Gruuthuse* next."

As the girls left the shop, however, Nancy sensed that somone was watching them. Across the street stood a man in a raincoat and hat. He glanced at the girl detectives, then disappeared down the street and around a corner.

Wondering if he had been waiting for them, Nancy decided not to mention this to the others until the pleasant tour was over.

Hilda, meanwhile, directed them to the large old building with minaretlike towers and a store facade. "This used to be the home of the Gruuthuse family. By our standards, it was a palace more than a house."

Inside, the visitors were impressed by the beautiful tapestries, china, and furniture. "How do you like these old beds?" Hilda asked when they reached the second floor. "Notice they are short and narrow. In the old days many people were small."

"Guess they didn't take their vitamins." George laughed.

Bess followed Hilda to the top floor where the Lace Room was. "What gorgeous centerpieces!" she exclaimed, gaping at the large display case. "It would be a real shame to put one of those on a table and then cover it up with a lamp or something."

Nancy was equally awestruck by the collection of lace collars. They were designed to stand up stiffly around the neck, some up to six inches high!

"Those are ruffs," Hilda explained. "They were very fashionable all over Europe in the seventeenth century."

George flinched. "I'd hate to wear one of those. They must have been very hot and uncomfortable."

There were also handmade children's dresses, hats, and handkerchiefs on exhibit. "Several of these things," Hilda remarked, observing Bess's admiring glance, "are worth many thousands of dollars—they are irreplaceable."

"Oh, my goodness!" Bess said. "And I was just

thinking how nice it would be to buy one to show everybody at home."

Hilda now suggested they go downstairs to see the guillotine. Bess trailed after her down the stairway while Nancy hung back, talking to George.

"Don't turn around," Nancy said in a low tone. "There's someone in this room who's been following us. I don't want to lose him."

"Well, you won't if he's following us," George said wryly.

She and Nancy stepped out of the room for a moment and pinned themselves against the outside wall behind the door. Surely the man would go downstairs now. The next few minutes ticked by slowly as the young detectives waited.

"You were wrong," George whispered to her friend when the stranger did not appear.

Nancy peered through the crack below the door hinge. "He's gone!" she cried, racing back into the empty room. Her eyes circled quickly to a balcony doorway. "He must have escaped through there!"

She dashed toward the opening and peered over the railing. Hand over hand, the man was lowering himself on a rope!

"He stole some of the lace!" the young detective gasped, seeing fringes of ruffles sticking out of his pockets.

Instinctively she leaned across the balcony and

grabbed the rope, pulling on it as hard as she could. But the man's weight was too much for her to budge. Suddenly Nancy's foot slipped and she lost her balance. She slid forward over the railing, ready to tumble over the edge!

# 13

## The Thief

Instantly George rushed toward Nancy and grabbed her around the waist, pulling her back fast. "That man mustn't get away!" Nancy cried.

But the thief was already halfway down the rope and was now dangling only a dozen feet above the ground.

"Oh, look! The rope's splitting!" George cried out.

Indeed, the strands were fraying rapidly until the last few threads snapped and the man hit the ground hard. His legs gave way underneath him, and he fell, letting out a howl of anguish.

"We're about to lose him!" George exclaimed, watching the thief try to get up.

"Maybe not," Nancy said. "He seems to have

hurt his ankle. Let's hurry downstairs. Chances are he won't be able to run away!"

The girl detectives flew down the stairway toward the front door and rushed around the building. Hilda and Bess, who were in the Weapons Room, were unaware of what had happened and wondered why their friends were taking so long to join them.

When Nancy and George reached the spot where the frayed rope lay, the man was gone.

"There he is!" George shouted, pointing to the thief as he desperately hobbled toward a bridge spanning a narrow canal between the *Gruuthuse* and another museum. Nancy darted ahead of her companion, yelling at the top of her lungs.

"Stop! *Arrêtez! Halt!*" But he kept limping on as fast as he could.

Halfway across the bridge, however, he paused to rest his hurt ankle. Nancy dived toward him, grabbing the lace centerpiece hanging out of his pocket. Instinctively, he snatched it back, causing the beautiful piece to tear in half!

"Get away from me!" he shouted at Nancy in English. Then he scooped her up in his arms, ready to push her over the stone railing into the water!

"Stop!" Nancy exclaimed just as George caught up to the pair and seized the man's arms.

Should she give him a judo flip into the canal?

No, she decided. He would drag Nancy along with him.

Instead, George continued to hold him while Nancy slid from his grasp and began to empty his pockets that were bulging with lace. Angrily, the man shoved the girls aside and darted across the bridge.

Her arms full of beautiful lace, Nancy called out, "George, go after him while I take this stuff back to the museum!"

George nodded and rushed after the man. Just as he stepped off the bridge, a group of visitors arrived, completely filling the narrow walkway. All of them were young men, laughing and joking with one another. When George tried to push past them, one caught her in his arms.

"Don't run away, pretty girl!" he said in a lilting Irish brogue. "Why don't you join us on our tour? We'd love to have something lovely to look at!"

"Please excuse me!" George said, trying to get away from him.

"Ye look like ye're running away from someone," another fellow said.

"No, I'm running *after* someone!" George cried in utter frustration. "A thief, if you want to know. Now please let me pass!"

The young man looked at her with big eyes. "A thief!"

By now George had wriggled out of his grip and slipped past the other young men. In a few long leaps, she crossed the bridge.

There was a narrow alley to her right and a park-like courtyard to her left. The man was nowhere in sight!

Some distance ahead of her was the other museum. Would he try to hide in there? George wondered. If I were he, where would I go?

In answer to her own question, she raced down the narrow street. But when she turned the next corner, there was no sign of the fugitive. Disgusted, George walked back to the museum. I've lost him, she said to herself. What bad luck!

She met Nancy in the lobby, surrounded by guards. They were excitedly jabbering in Flemish, and the woman from the reception desk walked up and translated for the girls.

"You stole these things from the exhibit upstairs!" she accused Nancy.

"I didn't steal anything!" the girl dectective said evenly. "Someone else did. He let himself down from the balcony on a rope. I caught him and got all the stuff back. But one piece ripped when he tried to hold on to it!"

The guards continued to converse loudly. Finally the woman said, "Jacques here said he saw you walking *into* the lobby with the lace, not running away with it. Will you please tell us exactly what happened?"

Nancy did, and George verified her explanation. Bess and Hilda, meanwhile, had left the Weapons Room and were looking for their friends. They were just in time to hear Nancy's story.

"Did he take the pieces from the glass display cases?" Nancy asked as she finished.

The receptionist shook her head. "No. We just received a new shipment which Jacques was bringing upstairs. Apparently the thief saw him and decided it would be easy to steal as long as he could get the guard out of the room."

"How did he manage that?" Bess asked.

"He told Jacques he was wanted in the lobby. So the unsuspecting guard put the box of lace behind one of the display cases and hurried downstairs. The thief then must have waited until you girls left the room before he made his next move and escaped over the balcony."

"But what about the rope?" George asked. "If he hadn't planned to steal the lace before he arrived, where'd he get the rope from?"

"Unfortunately, it was lying on a chest of drawers in one corner of the room," the receptionist said. "We had men working on the chimney, and they forgot to take the rope when they left early this morning before the museum opened. The thief saw it and realized it was long enough to help him down from the balcony."

The receptionist turned to Nancy. "What did the thief look like? I will call the police and ask them to look for him."

"He was tall and thin," Nancy said, "and wore a raincoat. He had a hat pulled low over his forehead, so I couldn't see his eyes too well. But his face was narrow, his lips thin, and his coloring was very pale, almost gray. He looked like a man who rarely went outdoors."

"He also limps because he hurt his ankle," George added.

"Thank you," the woman said. "I shall pass this information on to the authorities. Will you give me your names and addresses in case the police find the man and need to get in touch with you?"

The girls provided the information and then stepped out into the sunlight again.

"Phew, what an experience!" George said.

"That man was watching us at the Lace Center," Nancy told her friends. "He must have followed us all the way from there. I didn't want to say anything before, because I wasn't sure and didn't want to worry you. He might have been the same man who stole my suitcase at the airport. I didn't see his face then, but he had the same build as the lace thief."

"But if he wanted to know what we were up to, why would he draw attention to himself the way he did?" Bess asked.

"Perhaps he thought the cuffs with the message in them were among the antique lace pieces the guard brought upstairs for display," Nancy guessed.

"Well, unfortunately he got away," Hilda said. "There is nothing we can do about it. We might as well continue our tour." She paused briefly. "We'll go to an art museum—yes, I know just the one!"

The gallery she had in mind was filled with numerous paintings that depicted life in Brugge since the sixteenth century.

"As your father said, Hilda, not many things have changed, have they?" Nancy commented.

"No, they haven't. But we love the old charm of our city."

Suddenly an oil painting caught Nancy's eye. It was a striking portrait of a gallant young man with a mustache. He was wearing a red velvet jacket with a lace jabot and cuffs.

"Bess! George!" Nancy called out. "Look over here!"

Eagerly the girls joined her. "My goodness, that looks just as I imagined François Lefèvre." Bess gaped in surprise.

"But who's that behind him?" George asked.

In the scene the handsome young man was posed on an arched stone bridge. He was leaning forward, his hands on the edge of it. In back of him was the menacing shadow of another figure. Cloaked in a full black-hooded robe that covered his face and body completely, he was peering over the young man's shoulder. Two hands emerging from under the robe were ready to attack the unsuspecting victim.

"I wonder who the artist is," Bess said.

"There's no name on the picture, only initials," Nancy replied, "but maybe Hilda can tell us what they mean."

The Belgian girl said she was not familiar with this particular painting. "I've been here many times but I don't recall ever seeing it." Aloud she read the small gold plate underneath the picture. "*Le Cavalier et le Spectre Noir*. Translated that means *The Cavalier and the Black Ghost*. It must be a rather recent acquisition."

When she asked the curator, he replied, "It was found in somebody's attic. So far as I know, the museum did not pay very much money for it."

"Do you happen to know who sold it to the museum?" Nancy inquired.

The curator rubbed his chin with uncertainty. "Mm—no I don't, but even if I did I would not be able to answer your question. The museum keeps information about its purchases strictly confidential."

"Well, then," George put in, "perhaps you can tell us who the painter is."

"Yes. It was done by a man named Dirk Gelder, a well-known art teacher in his day. The story goes that the cavalier's girlfriend commissioned the painting, because her beau was an ardent admirer of Gelder."

"Do you know her name?" Nancy asked eagerly.

The curator shook his head. "Sorry. Now, if you'll excuse me," he said, "I have some business to attend to." He turned on his heels and walked away.

"Did you hear that?" George said excitedly. "The man in this picture was an admirer of Gelder, and so was François Lefèvre! I'll bet they're one and the same person!"

"If so," Bess added, "perhaps there's a hidden clue in the artwork that would help unravel the secret in the lace cuffs!"

Nancy nodded eagerly. She opened her handbag, took out her magnifying glass, and trained it on the lace cuffs.

"There's a clue in one of these cuffs!" she exclaimed.

# 14

## A Threat

"What's the message, Nancy?" Bess asked eagerly.

"Here, look for yourself," the girl detective replied, handing the magnifying glass to her friend.

"Oh, I see it!" Bess exclaimed, playing the glass over the lace cuff. "It says, *'Je vous aime.'* "

"Doesn't that mean 'I love you' in French?" George asked Hilda.

Hilda nodded, causing Bess to look dreamy-eyed. "How romantic!"

Nancy, in the meantime, was studying the intricate pattern in the lacework. Woven around the words was a scene of some sort. A geometric figure seemed to be the focal point. It was oblong with vertical stitches that curled into a knot at the top. Above the figure was a diagonal design that formed a baseless triangle. Nancy thought it was very strange.

"Is there anything in the other cuff?" George asked.

Nancy shook her head. "Unfortunately, the details are blurred. Maybe the artist deliberately chose not to paint them."

"Remember the piece of paper that was found in François's bedroom fireplace," George reminded her friends. "Wasn't the word *marry* on it?"

"So possibly the same word appears in the other cuff," Nancy said. "Of course, there must be more than one word. Perhaps the message was 'Marry me' or 'Don't marry anyone else.' "

"Or," Bess suggested, " 'Will you marry me?' "

"Or 'Marry Harry?' " George snickered.

Soon they were all laughing so hard the curator asked them to be quiet or leave. Hilda was already eyeing the door.

"My mother and father want all of you and Madame Chambray to come to dinner at eight o'clock," Hilda told her new friends. "Afterward, we'll watch the procession on the canal. Does that sound all right to you?"

"Oh, how exciting!" Bess replied promptly.

When the girls returned to Madame Chambray's house, there was only a short time to bathe, dress, and exchange news. Madame Chambray had found her desk key and used the opportunity to show the girls the letter she had written to Mrs. Marvin about.

The paper was yellow and splitting apart in the folds so Nancy held it carefully under a lamp. All that remained readable was part of a sentence, written in French, which Madame Chambray translated.

"I, Friedrich Vonderlicht, also known as François Lefèvre, leave to my wife, Elaine Warrington, the treasures of my family protected by our golden—"

Nancy stared at Madame Chambray. "Where did you find this?" she asked.

"Under a loose floorboard in one of the bedrooms."

George shook her head incredulously. "Isn't it odd," she said, "that none of the previous owners of this house ever discovered the will?"

"Not so odd," Madame Chambray replied. "I only came upon it because I was having the old floors refinished. The vibration of the sanding machine moved the loose section a little. I was helping the man who was about to nail it back into place when I noticed something yellowish underneath."

As she spoke, Nancy and George continued to study the document closely. "What are you thinking?" George asked her detective friend.

"The name Elaine Warrington sounds very familiar to me. Wasn't she a well-known actress in her day?" Nancy replied.

"I believe she was," Madame Chambray said.

"In that case," Bess declared, "we ought to be able to find out about her easily. Maybe she was married to François!"

"I wish we could start looking into that right now, but we've really got to get ready for dinner." Nancy sighed. They all agreed, and a short time later were seated in the Permeke home while the professor entertained the Americans with more historical stories about Brugge.

"Did you know," he asked, "that the *Gruuthuse* where you were today was once the refuge and hiding place of an English king?" Dr. Permeke explained that King Edward IV of England was forced into exile there for political reasons.

"Speaking of our tour," Nancy said, "we saw a most interesting portrait at one of the galleries."

Hilda repeated the name of the picture in French. "Joseph, have you heard of it?" she asked the student, who had joined the group for dinner.

"Yes. I believe it was painted by a man named Dirk Gelder. A young Frenchwoman, who was a friend of the man in the painting, asked him to do it."

"That's just what the curator told us," George

113

remarked. "Do you remember her name?"

"I read it somewhere," Joseph said. "Tissot—yes, that's it. Antoinette Tissot."

Nancy, Bess, and George were struck with the same startling thought. Was she not the same person whose name was stitched on the linen wrapping around the diamond cross?

"Do you know anything else about Antoinette Tissot?" Nancy inquired.

Joseph shook his head. "No. Sorry. I only saw her name in an article I once read about the painting."

Nancy's mind was racing. Perhaps Antoinette had given François the cross! If so, it now belonged to his descendants. But where were they? First thing the next morning, she and her friends would check the local telephone directory.

"There is another famous picture," Dr. Permeke told his guests. "The subject is a stout gentleman wearing breeches which just covered his knees. He has on long white stockings and at the top of them is a three-inch flounce of lace! Can you imagine dancing with him?"

Peals of laughter rang across the table. Bess, however, stopped giggling abruptly when the Permekes' housemaid placed a plate of eels in green sauce in front of her. The girl lifted her eyes from the dish and turned to her cousin. George was smirking.

"I dare you to try them!" George whispered in Bess's ear.

Bess poked her fork into the slippery meat, cutting off a small portion and popping it into her mouth. "It's delicious," she announced with a gulp.

Later, when everyone was seated at the edge of the canal waiting for the procession to pass by, Bess admitted to her friends, "I hope we don't have to eat again tonight. I'm not feeling very well."

"It's all in your mind," George said.

"Uh-uh, it's in my stomach."

The rest of Bess's remark was lost in the din of motorboats chugging past. Each craft was decorated with strings of lights rigged from pole to pole. Passengers on board wore all kinds of costumes, among them clowns, giants, monkeys, robbers, and even Dracula.

"Some of them are really scary," Bess commented, as another boat swung into view.

A ghostly figure was standing near the helm. He was completely covered by a sheet, only his feet were sticking out, and in his hand he held a small package.

Bess laughed. "Look, a ghost in cowboy boots!" she said, pointing to the man's footgear.

"He reminds me of that creep in Madame Chambray's basement," George declared. "He wore boots, too, only it was too dark to see much of them."

Soon the craft swerved close to the canal edge where the girl detectives sat and the strange figure hurled the package toward them. It fell a couple of feet away from them.

"I'll get it," Hilda volunteered. As she picked it up, she glanced at the writing on it. "Nancy, your name is on this!"

"My name?" the girl replied in surprise.

Quickly she opened the package. Inside was a small toy dagger and a note printed in bold letters.

"What's wrong?" Hilda's father asked, seeing the deepening frown on the detective's face.

"It says, 'Stop interfering or you will get this,' " Nancy said.

"How dreadful!" Madame Chambray exclaimed.

Everyone began talking at once and hardly noticed Nancy excuse herself and follow the route of the slow-moving boats in hopes of catching up with the ghostly stranger.

She hurried along the towpath and through the adjoining park that bordered the canal which curved just ahead of her. For a moment she lost sight of the boat, but caught up to it a few minutes later. Suddenly she gasped. The mysterious ghost had vanished!

"Where is your passenger?" the young sleuth

asked the boatman as she ran alongside his craft.

"I do not know," he replied in halting English. "He made me pull over and jumped out."

"Thank you," Nancy said in disappointment, and hurried back to her group.

When they heard her report, Dr. Permeke suggested that Madame Chambray lock all the windows and doors in her house. "And please," the professor urged, "do not go out of your house alone."

Everyone agreed that was a good idea. Madame Chambray and her young guests thanked the Permekes for the delightful evening and took a taxi home. Upon arriving at the house, they discovered an open window on the first floor.

"I don't understand it," Madame Chambray said. "I'm sure I closed everything before we left." Fearfully she slipped her key into the front door lock.

"Let me go in first," Nancy suggested.

Cautiously she stepped into the hallway. A lamp was burning dimly in the living room. At first glance none of Madame Chambray's belongings were missing, but everything looked slightly out of place to Nancy. Thinking of the diamond cross hidden in a corner cabinet, Nancy ran up to it and opened the middle drawer. The purple velvet box was missing!

117

# 15

## Cowboy Suspect

The diamond cross was stolen! Heartsick, Madame Chambray crumpled into a chair. "It's all my fault. I was so stupid to tell the newspaper about it!"

While Bess and George tried to comfort her, Nancy darted to the telephone and called the police. She gave a full report of the theft and the earlier events of the evening.

"I'm positive that the man who threw the package at me stole the antique cross," she said.

The *politieagent* at the other end promised to send a patrol to the area immediately. Before going to bed, Nancy checked her bureau drawer for the old document Madame Chambray had entrusted to her. Fortunately, it was still there.

Nancy had much to report when her father

phoned the next morning. Upon hearing the name Elaine Warrington, he said, "She appeared in some very fine plays in this country in the late eighteen hundreds. I may be able to track down some information about her for you, if you like."

"Oh would you, Dad?" Nancy asked gratefully. "Then all I'll have left to do is figure out what the mysterious something is that's mentioned in the will!"

"By the way," her father went on, "Mr. Miller from *Circle and Square* magazine told me that the unfriendly editor, Herbert Rocke, left New York a few days ago to go on vacation."

"I have a feeling that he intercepted the first copy of my manuscript," Nancy declared.

"I'm sure he did, because Mr. Miller found out that Rocke is a friend of your contest rival, Mr. Frieden!"

"What!"

"Of course, the magazine would never have permitted a friend of one of its editors to participate in the contest; but as Mr. Miller said, he didn't know of the connection until recently. Anyway, Miller has been trying to reach Mr. Frieden about his entry ever since he saw you but hasn't been able to."

"Interesting," Nancy said. "Rocke must have given Frieden my original to copy and submit to the magazine as his own."

"Nancy," Mr. Drew said slowly, "a lot of these

things don't make sense. Why would Rocke and Frieden get involved in something like that? There's no big money to be made. Other factors must be involved that we don't know about yet. That's why I want you to be very careful."

"What do you mean, Dad?"

"It's possible both Frieden and Rocke might turn up in Brugge. I want you to watch out for them."

"What do they look like?"

"I don't know about Frieden, but Rocke is tall and thin, with a narrow face and thin lips. His complexion is very pale."

"That's the man who followed us from the Lace Center and then stole the new shipment from the *Gruuthuse!*" Nancy exclaimed.

"He may be," Mr. Drew said cautiously. "Unfortunately, I can't send you a photograph for a more positive identification. Are the police looking for this man?"

"Yes. I gave the people at the museum a good description."

"I'm glad," Mr. Drew said. "And I have another piece of information you'll be interested in."

"What's that?"

"Frieden's address is the same as André Bergère's."

"Oh, dear!" Nancy cried out. "Maybe they know

each other and Frieden read Madame Chambray's letter to Mrs. Marvin!"

"It's quite possible. So please be extra careful!"

After Hilda arrived that morning, Nancy confided her father's report to everyone.

"So Rocke's the lace thief!" George declared.

"And maybe the ghost who threw the dagger," Bess added, "and stole the diamond cross!"

"Or," Nancy pointed out, "Frieden or Bergère could be the culprit!"

Despite the recent theft, Nancy decided to find out if any descendants of François Lefèvre were living in Brugge. A quick scan of the local telephone directory revealed nothing.

"Dad's going to let me know what he can about Elaine Warrington, but I thought we ought to do some digging ourselves about her," Nancy said. "Why don't we go to the library and see if we can find anything?"

"Good idea," George and Bess agreed.

On the way to the library, Nancy noticed a tall man peering into a shop window. He was wearing a ten-gallon hat and a well-tailored cowboy suit. On his feet were beautiful leather boots much like the ones worn by the ghostly intruder!

"Come on!" Nancy told her friends and hurried toward the man.

"Hello! You're from the United States, aren't

you?" Nancy asked boldly. "So are we."

"Well, I'm sure glad to meet you all," the cowboy replied, extending his hand to shake theirs.

"We've been here a few days," Nancy said. "When did you arrive?"

"Only a little while ago. I flew in with a charter group."

The man seemed genuinely friendly. Either the girls' suspicions were unfounded or he was putting on an act!

"Your boots are pretty fancy," George said pointedly.

Still unflustered, the cowboy thanked her for the compliment. "They're straight from Dallas, like me."

"You don't by any chance know two men named Frieden and Rocke?" Bess asked.

The cowboy shook his head

George glared at her cousin for blurting out such revealing information. "Do you travel much?" she asked, changing the subject abruptly.

"Not a whole lot," he said, "but I may be doing some more if I land a part with a summer playhouse—" He stopped talking when a young woman emerged from the shop. She trotted past him, clearly annoyed. "Nice to meet you," he said quickly to the girls and hurried after the woman.

As they watched him disappear down the street,

Nancy wondered if he really was their suspect and if they should alert the police.

"If he changes his shoes and his outfit," George said, laughing, "they'll never find him."

The foursome headed for the library, and with Hilda's help found a large book about the history of the theater. Among the names listed in the index was Elaine Warrington's. There were several references to her, including mention of her marriage to Friedrich Vonderlicht after her family had disowned her.

"Where was she from?" Bess inquired.

"According to this," Nancy replied, "she was born in France but lived in the United States. Apparently she lived in Europe most of her married life but returned to America abruptly after her husband's death and died penniless—so she must not have known about François's will or the treasure."

"Or if she did, she never found it, or maybe he died while she was on tour, and he never had a chance to tell her," George said. "Was Warrington her real name?"

"I doubt it," Nancy replied, shutting the book. "It must've been her stage name."

"And François must have changed his name to Vonderlicht when he settled in Brugge!" Bess declared.

"Well," Nancy replied, "let's go back to Madame

123

Chambray's house. Some of the answers have got to be hidden there."

Hilda admitted she had never done any detective work before but was eager to help. She even agreed to search the basement where the ghostly intruder had captured Bess.

"You go ahead," Bess said. "I have no desire to be thrown into a closet again."

"You won't," George insisted. "We locked the tunnel door so no one can get in there."

"Even so, I prefer to stay up here in the safety of the kitchen."

"You just want to be near the refrigerator," her cousin teased, following Nancy and Hilda down the cellar steps. They had found extra flashlights and beamed them ahead as they descended.

Fascinated by the depth of the room, Hilda said, "Centuries ago I imagine this place was filled with boxes and barrels of food. People used to import it from many parts of the world—luscious bananas from the warmer climates and olives, too—"

Her light now shone on the tunnel door, prompting Nancy to interrupt.

"George, wasn't there a key in that door?"

"Yes."

"Well, it's gone."

George hurried forward and turned the handle. The door swung back freely.

Distressed, Nancy examined it for evidence of force. "The door isn't damaged; it's been unlocked with a key. But how? Did someone enter the basement from upstairs or from the tunnel?"

"There's no way to tell," George said.

"But I'm sure it was Mr. Ghost again!"

Hilda expressed alarm as well. "No one in this house is safe!" she said.

# 16

## Exciting Clue

While the other girls were in the cellar, Bess decided to do her own investigating, but was at a loss as to where to begin. She remembered seeing a door at the end of the hall on the second floor and, not knowing if it led to the third story or another closet, concluded she'd start there.

Bess shivered nervously as she approached the door. "I refuse to be called 'Chicken Marvin' any more," she murmured, opening the door.

Before her was a twist of stairs that rose steeply upward toward a small landing. She took a few steps, then paused, listening to a shuffling noise above her. It sounded as though someone was in the room overhead.

Bess froze temporarily but continued the climb. To her surprise there was no door at the top—only a window opposite an unevenly papered wall.

Hmph, that's odd, the young detective thought. A bunch of steps that lead nowhere!

She pressed her ear against the wall. The shuffling sounds had stopped, at least for the moment.

It must have been my imagination, Bess concluded, turning to leave.

But suddenly she felt something settle on her forehead. It moved, tickling her skin. Quickly she brushed it to the floor, shrieking and jumping flat against the wall as a spider crawled into a corner. At the same time Bess's hand detected a crack in the wood. Was it the work of termites or of an eccentric architect? she wondered.

Curiously, the girl sleuth ran her fingers along the depression. The wallpaper crackled as it tore apart—revealing a panel!

Bess's heart pounded hard. She tugged at the wood but it was warped. Now what'll I do? She sighed, her mind racing. Well, at least, I know one thing. If I can't get through this wall, Mr. Ghost couldn't either!

She flew downstairs to the kitchen, shouting to her friends in the cellar. They rejoined her immediately and told her about the missing key to the tunnel door.

"Uh-oh," Bess said. "Then maybe there is some-body upstairs." She revealed her discovery and the shuffling sounds on the third floor.

The girls locked the door between the kitchen and the cellar in order to prevent an intrusion through the tunnel. Then, armed with flashlights and a thin steel wedge they found in an old tool-box, the young sleuths followed Bess upstairs. Nancy worked the wedge deftly into the crack in the wall, forcing the panel back slightly.

"It's coming," she said, and stuck her fingers through the opening.

George and Hilda placed their hands around the wood as well. Inch by inch they moved it back. "There's another wall behind this one!" George ex-claimed as Madame Chambray's familiar voice called to them from below.

"Girls!" she shouted. "Where are you?"

Bess hurried down to the second floor landing. "We're up here! We found a hidden panel!" she called loudly.

"I'll be right there," the woman said, dropping the packages she had brought.

When she saw the partly open wall, the torn pa-per and steel wedge, Madame Chambray gasped. "What are you doing?"

"We think there's a hidden room on the other side of this wall," Nancy explained.

"A hidden room? How interesting. How did you find it?"

Bess explained how she had discovered the crack. "That spider really was helpful, even though I hate the things." she concluded.

"Well, someday I'll have to explore that room," Mrs. Chambray said.

"I think we should do it right now," Nancy urged. "The treasure might be hidden in there!"

Madame Chambray nodded absentmindedly, and Nancy wondered why the woman did not share the girls' excitement. Instead, she almost seemed sad.

"We might even discover a clue to the owner of the diamond cross!" Nancy went on.

"I've found him already," Madame Chambray said.

"You have? Where—"

Nancy was interrupted by the ringing of the telephone. It was Mr. Drew.

"Hi, Dad," Nancy said. "Any news?"

Nancy listened eagerly as her father told her his startling discovery. A relative of Elaine Warrington, her great-grandson in fact, was traveling in Belgium!

"That's fantastic!" Nancy exclaimed. "What's his full name—of course, his family name is Vonderlicht."

"He changed it to Vaughan . . . Cody Vaughan," Mr. Drew said.

Nancy laughed. "He sounds like a cowboy," she said.

"He is. Well, not exactly. He's an actor who's been working at different jobs to prepare for roles he hopes to get. He moved to Dallas not long ago—"

"I think," Nancy cut in excitedly, "we may already have met Mr. Vaughan!"

She told her father about the cowboy they had spoken to in town, then added, "But Madame Chambray claims she's found the owner of the antique cross."

"Did she say who he is?"

"No. We were interrupted by the phone."

"Well, maybe she ran into Mr. Vaughan also," Mr. Drew said. "Let me know what's happening, Nancy, and take care of yourself."

"I will, Dad."

After the girl hung up, she found Madame Chambray in the living room with her face buried in her hands. Nancy darted to her side, slipping one arm around the woman's shoulder.

"What's the matter, Madame Chambray?" She asked softly. "Don't you feel well?"

The woman lifted her eyes dolefully. "You must leave this house at once, dear," she said. "It isn't safe for you to stay here any longer."

Nancy sensed that something had happened that was troubling Madame Chambray a great deal.

"Has someone threatened you?" she inquired.

"N-no."

"Are you sure?"

"No, I mean, yes, I—uh . . ."

"Madame Chambray, we can't leave you alone," the young sleuth said. "Please tell me what is bothering you."

The other girls kept silent, allowing the woman to speak. Haltingly she said, "This came in the mail."

She pulled a letter from her skirt pocket and handed it to Nancy, who read it aloud. "Dear Madame, your visitors have put a curse on your house. They must leave immediately or it will burn!"

"This is only an empty threat," Nancy said.

"How do you know?" Bess spoke up.

"It sounds like a real one to me," Hilda agreed.

"But this is a stone house," Nancy retorted. "No one can burn it."

"Not the shell, perhaps," Madame Chambray said, wiping her eyes. "But inside there is wood everywhere. Oh, you must go back to America! I cannot be responsible for your safety any longer."

The girls begged the woman to reconsider but she remained firm. "Besides, someone called me just before I left here today. He claims to be the

131

owner of the diamond cross. He's coming here later."

"But the cross is gone," Bess observed.

"I told him that. But he still wants to see me," the woman replied.

"Did he give his name?" Nancy asked.

"No."

"Did he speak with a Texan drawl?"

"No."

"Then I'm positive he's an impostor!" the girl detective said resolutely.

# 17

## *Hidden Treasure?*

"Madame Chambray," the girl detective said, trying a new tack to convince the anxious woman to let them stay, "I believe the secret in the old lace is buried here. If you want us to leave tomorrow, we will; but please give us till then to continue our search."

The woman did not answer immediately. She glanced at the pleading expression on her visitors' faces, then spoke. "All right, you have until tomorrow, but for your own sakes, I can't permit you to—"

"Oh, thank you!" Nancy interrupted, hugging her.

George sighed. "I hate to admit defeat," she said,

"But if François Lefèvre's secret has been hidden for more than a century, how can we find it in less than twenty-four hours?"

"Think positive!" Nancy grinned.

Reluctantly Madame Chambray gave permission for the girls to open the panel on the third floor. "I suppose I ought to put new wallpaper up there anyway," she said.

"I'm sorry I won't be able to stay and help you," Hilda spoke up. "But Joseph is taking me to a concert this evening. Perhaps all of you would like to join us . . . if this is to be your last evening in Brugge."

"We would love to," Bess said, "but it sounds as if Nancy has other plans for us."

The girls thanked Hilda for her invitation but said they expected to spend every minute left on the mystery. After saying good-bye, they hurried upstairs, and in less than half an hour slid the double panel fully open.

Beyond, drenched in sunlight streaming through a skylight, was a strange-looking room framed by high beams. It was cluttered with antique furniture, china, pictures, knickknacks of all kinds, and an old trunk thick with dust like everything else.

"What should we tackle first?" George asked, spying a pile of boxes in a corner.

"That's exactly what I was going to ask," her

cousin replied. "Maybe we ought to split up our investigation."

Bess headed toward a delicate silk screen that stood near the center of the room, and peered behind it. On the floor lay an old tarnished birdcage which she set upright.

"Find anything of interest?" George called out from her corner of the room.

"Uh-uh, just a birdcage without a bird."

Nancy, in the meantime, was drawn to the big trunk. She raised the lid, revealing bundles of newspapers and letters.

"These are all addressed to François!" Bess observed excitedly. She opened one of them. "Here's an invitation to a ball in Brussels! Oh, I wish I could've gone too. It must've been fabulous!"

"And this is an invitation to a big party," George said, pulling out another letter. "I'd say François had a terrific social life!"

As the girls continued to sift through the papers, Nancy suddenly discovered a leather-bound book beneath them.

"Look, I've just found his diary!" she exclaimed and read several passages aloud, translating them from French into English.

Bess hung on every word, gazing moonstruck toward the skylight where a face pulled suddenly out of sight!

"Oh!" the girl gasped, causing her friends to look at the window.

"What is it?" Nancy asked.

"A-a man—" Bess stuttered.

"You're imagining things," her cousin said. "There's no one—"

"But I saw him—"

Nancy laid the diary on the pile of papers in the trunk and slid a chair under the skylight. "I don't see anybody," she said, after climbing on the chair. "But the skylight isn't locked. I wonder if someone's been using it as his access to the attic. He could have made the noise Bess heard."

"We should report this to the police," George suggested, and left to make the call.

Meanwhile, Nancy read more of the diary. It revealed that François was in love with an actress. "And guess who she was?" Nancy asked.

"Elaine Warrington, of course," Bess said.

"Uh-uh. It was Antoinette Tissot!"

"What! But I thought he married Elaine Warrington."

"He did," Nancy said. "Originally her name was Antoinette. It seems that her family disapproved not only of her interest in François but also of her desire to become an actress. I guess they thought François was a playboy and insisted Antoinette not see him. She refused to obey."

Nancy read and translated one of the passages. " 'I cannot permit her to be disowned. I can't do it. I'm going to disappear and change my name. François Lefèvre will be no more.' "

"Amazing," George broke in. She had overheard the girls' conversation as she climbed the stairs. "I gather Antoinette followed François to Brugge—"

"And changed her name to Elaine Warrington when she joined an acting troupe," Nancy said, "since she did not wish to disgrace her family name."

"But if she and François got married," Bess went on, "why didn't Antoinette simply work under his new name?"

"Because they didn't get together right away," Nancy answered. "According to this diary, François tried to send her back to her family—"

"But she was in love with him," Bess sighed. "Isn't it wonderful?"

Meanwhile, Nancy continued to flip through the book and settled on another long passage. "Joseph Stolk was right," she said. "Antoinette did ask Dirk Gelder to paint that picture of François. It symbolized the end of Monsieur Lefèvre. From then on, he would be known as Friedrich Vonderlicht."

Bess opened a fair-sized box near the trunk. "Look, everybody!" she exclaimed, holding up a red velvet cavalier suit with a lace jabot and

138

detachable lace cuffs. "This must have been François's!"

Excited, Nancy dashed to Bess and took the
cuffs, examining them inch by inch. They were intricately woven, but to the girls' chagrin, there was
no message in either of them.

"They are beautiful nonetheless," Nancy said,
dropping the cuffs back in the box.

Now she picked up the diary once again, wondering if she had overlooked anything else of interest. A few pages from the end she discovered a
description of a beautiful statue in a tiny walled-in
garden, and tied to the last page with pale blue
ribbon was a painting of a man with a golden face
and hair. He was wearing a close-fitting gold suit.
One hand rested on a low pedestal fountain in the
garden.

"Maybe this is where the treasure is hidden!"
Nancy exclaimed. "The will mentioned it was protected by something golden!"

When she told Madame Chambray about her
discovery, the woman said, "I know where that
statue is. It's right here on the grounds!"

She led the way to a small garden behind the
house. In the center stood a gold statue!

"May we move it to see if anything is buried underneath?" Bess asked Madame Chambray.

The woman nodded slowly. "I will get some

tools," she said as the girls loosened the base by hand. Within moments the marble figure and pedestal had been pushed carefully aside and the girls had started digging.

"It's such an unlikely place to hide a treasure," Madame Chambray insisted. "After so many years, it would be ruined by now."

But the diggers continued, filled with anticipation. They failed to see a man peering over the garden wall. His snakelike eyes glistened eagerly as George's spade struck something hard.

"Hold everything!" she cried out.

All work stopped while George's fingers probed the dirt. She yanked on something, prying it free.

"A stone!" she exclaimed in disgust and threw it aside.

The work went on for several minutes until Nancy jabbed the soil hard with her shovel. Almost instantly water began to seep through the soil. She pulled the shovel out and a needle-sharp geyser shot up toward her face!

# 18

## The Spy

Quickly Nancy dodged the geyser of water. As she did, she happened to glance at the top of the garden wall. A man with shiny black hair was staring ominously at her. Was he the same person Bess had seen through the skylight? Before Nancy could attract her friend's attention, the spy slithered out of sight. Meanwhile, the groundwater continued to gush.

"I must have punctured a water pipe with my shovel," Nancy said to Madame Chambray. "I'm terribly sorry."

"I'll go and call the water department. I'm sure they can fix it." She went inside and returned shortly. "Someone is coming right away. But what should we do in the meantime?"

Instantly George jumped down into the hole and tried to hold her hand over the opening in the pipe.

"It won't work," she said, disappointed. "Bess, why don't you sit on it?"

"Very funny," her cousin replied.

Less jovial, Nancy watched the slow buildup of water. If this keeps up, she thought, it will saturate the entire garden and prevent us from unearthing the hidden treasure!

Within fifteen minutes, however, a repairman arrived, carrying a bag of tools. He turned the water off, then worked rapidly to replace the damaged section of pipe.

"That ought to do it," he said at last, shaking mud off his feet as he stepped on the stone path that circled the statue.

"How long do you think it will take the ground to dry?" Nancy asked.

"We're looking for buried treasure," Bess cut in.

The man looked surprised but did not inquire further. "Well, it will take a day or so for all the water to drain," he replied.

"Gracious!" George said. "We can't wait that long!"

After the repairman left, Nancy told the others about the spy whom she had noticed by the garden wall. "He may have been Frieden or Bergère. I'm pretty sure I'd recognize him if I saw him again."

"Maybe he wanted to steal my beautiful statue!" Madame Chambray declared.

"Well, we are going to catch him before he pulls a stunt like that," Bess said bravely.

Nancy grinned at her friend. "You always come through in a pinch!" she said.

The girls figured the suspect must have approached the garden from the back steps that led down to the canal. They followed the towpath, hoping to find evidence of the stranger. Was he hiding among trees or had he left in a boat?

Chugging some distance away was a small craft. The man at the wheel had sleek black hair. For an instant he shot a glance back at the house.

"That's the spy!" Nancy exclaimed, squinting to read the name painted on the boat. It was *Wit Bloem*.

"I wonder what it means," George said.

"Madame Chambray can tell us," Bess declared, following her friends back to the house.

When asked, the woman told the girls that *Wit Bloem* meant white flower. "But why do you wish to know?" she added.

Nancy explained about the man in the boat, prompting her hostess to call the police. She reported the incident and at Nancy's suggestion, requested the name and address of the boat's owner.

It seemed like hours before the *politie* telephoned back.

"The craft belongs to a man named Theo Schlinger," the voice said and gave the man's address.

Nancy suggested they ask Hilda to go with them to meet the man. "We may need a translator," she said.

"You mean we may need the police! Besides, Hilda's going to a concert with Joseph," Bess reminded Nancy.

"Well, maybe she can squeeze in one more favor beforehand, and anyway, I think we can handle Mr. Schlinger. We don't have to accuse him of anything." Hopeful, the young sleuth telephoned the girl and after several minutes of conversation put down the receiver, beaming.

"She can go with us if we don't stay long!" Nancy exclaimed.

An hour later the girls arrived at Mr. Schlinger's home, and, exchanging nervous smiles, knocked on the door. A moment later an elegant gentleman, not the thief, appeared. He proved to be as delightful as his home, which was filled with nautical souvenirs, pictures of old sailing ships, and a photograph of Mr. Schlinger in a boatman's cap.

"Do you speak English?" Nancy asked him.

"A little," he replied. "Why, are you interested in finding a tour guide?"

"Oh, no," Nancy laughed. "Miss Permeke has already taken us sightseeing. It was wonderful."

Hilda blushed at the compliment and said she would translate any of Nancy's questions that Mr. Schlinger did not understand.

"Sounds like you mean serious business," Mr. Schlinger said. "Perhaps you would like to rent my boat?"

"N-no," Nancy said. "But we'd like to know who was using it today."

"His name was Bergère," Mr. Schlinger said. "He took the boat for an hour or so, then brought it back."

"Bergère!" Nancy cried out. "That's the man we're looking for!"

"You are? Is there a problem?" Mr. Schlinger asked

"Yes," Nancy replied. "We believe that man is a thief!"

"Oh, dear," Mr. Schlinger said, running his hand through his hair. "If I had known that, I would never have permitted him to—"

"Did he by any chance give you his address?" Bess interrupted.

The boatman shook his head. "No. But he did tell me that this was his last day in Brugge, and that he was flying back to New York tonight."

Mr. Schlinger did not know anything else about Bergère's plans, so the girls thanked him and left.

On the way home they discussed their next move.

"Now I'm convinced that Matey Johnson showed Bergère the letter Madame Chambray wrote to Mrs. Marvin," Nancy said. "That's why he came here."

"But it wouldn't make sense for him to leave Brugge before finding the treasure, would it?" George spoke up.

"Unless he stole the diamond cross and figures that's enough to bring home for now," Bess suggested.

"True," Nancy said. "He could even be planning to return to Brugge after we leave." But her mind took another turn. "Still, I don't believe he would return to America and then fly all the way back to Belgium. He probably lied because he figured we saw the name on his boat and would trace it to Mr. Schlinger. Perhaps he had already given Mr. Schlinger his name and was afraid we would find out."

"Good thinking!" George praised her friend. "So he told the fib about returning to New York hoping we'd stop looking for him."

Hilda was glancing worriedly at her watch. "I really ought to be on my way," she said finally. "Where are you going now?"

"That's the big question," Bess said. "The airport or home?"

"Home," Nancy said decisively. "I want to meet that impostor when he shows up."

On the way, they passed by a series of shops, including a quaint bookshop. "I guess this will be our only chance to buy gifts to take home," Bess pointed out, ducking inside.

The girls selected beautiful books about Belgium for each of their boyfriends.

"Maybe this will get them to come with us next time," George said.

As they paid for their purchases, Nancy glanced at a glass display case. In the reflection was a large cowboy hat.

It was the young man from Texas who fit Mr. Drew's description of François's great-grandson!

# 19

## The Capture

Nancy whirled around to face the young Texan. "Cody Vaughan?" she asked, smiling broadly.

He flashed a grin at her and the other girls. "Mighty nice to see you all again," he said, "but how do you know my name? I never told you what it is."

Nancy introduced herself and her friends, then explained briefly, adding, "We've been hoping to run into you again. We're staying at a house that belonged to your great-grandparents."

"No kidding," the cowboy said. "I knew my family was originally from Belgium. That's one reason I decided to make this trip. It's my first time here, you know." He breathed in deeply. "Gee, I'd love to see that place."

"You will." Nancy sparkled. "Just wait until Madame Chambray meets you. She'll be so excited. She's been searching for a descendant of the Vonderlicht family."

"Who is Madame Chambray?" the fellow asked, puzzled. "And why on earth would she want to meet me?"

"She owns the Vonderlicht house now," Bess pointed out. "Shortly after she moved in, she found a beautiful antique cross wrapped in a piece of cloth that bore the name Antoinette Tissot—your great-grandmother."

"I think you folks have me mixed up with somebody. My great-grandmother's name wasn't Tissot. It was Warrington—Elaine Warrington."

Prompted to reveal the romantic story of Antoinette and François, George told how they moved to Brugge and changed their names.

"And they lived happily ever after," Bess finished.

"There's one small problem," Nancy put in soberly. "The diamond cross was stolen. But I have a hunch you can help us get it back!"

"Oh, I don't know, Nancy. I'm not much on catching crooks," Cody said. "On second thought, though, maybe it's not such a bad idea after all. I might get an acting part someday as a detective."

"Then you'll go to the house with us?" Nancy asked. "It's not very far from here."

She noticed that the young woman with whom she had seen him on the previous occasion was not in the store.

"Okay," Cody said, "but I'd like to call my hotel first. I have a date with somebody. Can she come along?"

Nancy hesitated, uncertain of the danger that might lay ahead of them. "Why don't you suggest meeting your friend a little later? You can call her from the house," Nancy said.

"I don't know how that'll set with her," the man said, "but I'll tell her."

By now, a haze of twilight covered the town, and there was a forbidding stillness in the air as the group reached the old stone house. To their surprise only one or two of the lamps were lit.

"Somebody's inside," Nancy said, seeing the outline of a man's head in the window.

"Should we knock?" Bess asked fearfully.

"No," Nancy replied, "we might scare off Madame Chambray's visitor."

She turned the door handle slowly, hoping it was not locked. The door clicked open. Signaling everyone to remain quiet, Nancy tiptoed inside. A murmur of words and laughter drifted into the hallway.

"Oh, Monsieur, I am so pleased to meet you at last," Madame Chambray was saying. "But, to tell the truth, I am very troubled."

"How could such a lovely lady be so troubled?" The man's voice oozed sweetly. It sounded vaguely familiar. "You know my grandfather had terrible troubles—romantic ones mostly. Women pursued him constantly. One girl from Brussels in particular literally forced him to move here to Brugge. She was simply too ardent."

"But," Madame Chambray said, "didn't he marry her?"

"Oh, no. He met somebody else."

Nancy's thoughts now fell clearly into place. That man was telling the story she had entered in the magazine contest! He was either Paul Frieden or André Bergère! She paused long enough for Bess to tug on her arm.

"I heard something upstairs," Bess whispered.

Was there another intruder in the house—a partner perhaps of the man seated inside? the girls wondered.

"What should we do?" George asked.

"You and Bess check the top floors while I introduce Cody to Madame Chambray," Nancy said.

Cautiously, Bess and George tiptoed to the second floor while the Texan trailed Nancy into the living room. The visitor was hidden from view in a high-backed chair.

"Excuse me, Madame Chambray," Nancy said politely, "but I'd like you to meet the great-grandson of François Lefèvre—"

"That's impossible!" the other man spouted angrily. He rose to his feet and turned sharply toward Nancy.

He was tall and slender, with a narrow face, thin lips, and a pallid complexion.

"Mr. Rocke!" Nancy cried out.

Furious, the man bolted past the girl, shoving her aside. "I don't know you," he growled.

"Grab him, Cody!" Nancy cried, but the agile impostor slipped out of the cowboy's reach.

He tripped on the carpet, causing a small, glittering object to fall out of his pocket. "It's the diamond cross!" Madame Chambray shouted.

Before Rocke could retrieve it, however, Nancy dived for it. He flew through the hallway, out the door, and down the steps to a waiting boat. Before Nancy or Cody Vaughan could catch him, he sped away.

"That's the last of Mr. Ghost," Nancy said, noticing the man's boots. "The only time he didn't wear those boots was when he followed us to the *Gruuthuse* and stole the lace!"

At once, the girl called the authorities and described Rocke and the boat he had escaped in. "He went up the canal in an easterly direction," she added.

"We'll look for him at once," the officer on duty promised. "We will also alert the airport. In case

he tries to leave the country, his passport will be flagged down."

Bess and George, in the meantime, were unaware of what had occurred below. Nothing was out of order on the second floor so they climbed to the third.

"I definitely heard something," Bess said, "and it's too far for mice to climb."

She and her cousin poised themselves outside the attic panel, then slowly slid it open. Except for the soft glow of streetlamps that traveled through the skylight, the room was completely dark.

"Stick close," George whispered.

"Don't worry." Bess shivered, beaming her flashlight toward the trunk and boxes.

"If someone was here," George observed, "I'm sure he left." A chair stood under the skylight. "And that's how he went."

As she swung her light to another corner, Bess noticed an antique bureau. All the drawers had been pulled out, revealing lace-trimmed garments and lots of books that resembled the leather-bound diary in the trunk.

"I don't recall that we ever opened those drawers," George said. "They don't have handles so we probably didn't realize they were drawers. The intruder must have pried them open."

"What about François's red jacket and the lace

154

cuffs?" Bess murmured. "I wonder if they were stolen?"

She hurried to the box near the trunk. The jacket was still there but the cuffs were gone! Obviously, the thief had mistaken them for the ones containing the secret message!

Suddenly the girls sensed that someone was behind them. Indeed, the hunched figure of a man was shuffling toward them, ready to pounce. In his hands were the missing lace cuffs.

"Help!" Bess cried aloud, as George gathered up all her courage and lunged toward the man.

Help, however, was on the way for the two terrified girls. Nancy and Cody leaped into the room, tackling the intruder. They pushed him to the floor within seconds.

"Let go of me!" he bellowed angrily.

"Not until the police come," Cody said, twisting the man's arm out flat.

"You're André Bergère, aren't you?" Nancy accused him, recognizing his face and sleek black hair. "I suppose Paul Frieden is around here as well."

Their captive laughed bitterly. Then, thinking he had everything under control, Cody loosened his grip a bit. Bergère took advantage of the movement, punching Cody in the ribs.

"Ow!" the Texan sputtered, allowing the prisoner to free himself in a sudden quick turn.

Nancy, however, grabbed his arm while George hooked another one, ready to heave him in a judo flip!

# 20

## A Double Surprise

Once again Cody joined the struggle, weakening their prisoner at last.

"Quick, call the police, Bess!" Nancy told the girl.

"Oh, don't do that! I beg you!" the man pleaded in exhaustion as Bess ran downstairs. His arms sank limply in those of his captors. "Just let me sit down a minute."

"Don't you try anything funny," Cody warned.

"I won't, I promise I won't," The intruder gulped for air. "What do you want to know?"

"Are you or are you not André Bergère?" Nancy questioned. Nervously he ran his bony fingers through his sleek black hair.

"I am and—"

"And what?" Nancy prodded.

"And Paul Frieden."

"What!" She stared at him in surprise. "You mean, Frieden is only a fictitious character?"

Bergère nodded.

"So when Rocke intercepted my manuscript," Nancy continued, "he passed it on to *you!*"

Bergère shrugged. "We're friends."

"Was the contest prize worth so much to you that you decided to plagiarize my story and submit it yourself?" Nancy asked, feeling a twinge of disgust for the man.

"We knew there was an unsolved mystery in Brugge, that's why we ran the contest," Bergère grumbled. "We figured if Miller accused *you* of plagiarism, you'd stick around New York until you convinced him otherwise. Meanwhile, we could come here and search for the treasure mentioned in the letter."

George chuckled. "You must have been surprised when you found out from Rocke that Nancy was going ahead with her travel plans."

"So you waited for me to arrive at the airport and then stole my luggage!" Nancy added.

"No. That was Rocke," Bergère protested. "He borrowed an airport worker's jacket so he could get past the guards with your bag."

"He wanted to stall me in Brussels for a while," Nancy said, "but when that didn't work out the way he planned, he decided to scare us. Rocke played ghost in Madame Chambray's house—"

"I also kept close watch on everything you did," the prisoner interrupted with a self-congratulatory smile. "I watched you in the garden and through the skylight and—"

"How did Rocke ever get the key to the tunnel?" Nancy went on.

"The first time he went there the door was open and the key was inside," Bergère replied. "He had a duplicate made."

"Once Rocke came when the door was locked from the inside," Nancy said, remembering the time she had left the key in the lock.

"He pushed it out with a stick, then used his duplicate," Bergère said. "These locks aren't hard to tamper with."

"Did Rocke have fun riding in the procession?" George asked. "You didn't really think that dagger trick would frighten us, did you?"

Bergère shrugged. "We were desperate. Unfortunately, nothing worked. You girls spoiled everything!"

Just then Madame Chambray and Bess appeared in the doorway with two policemen.

"Here's the man who sent you that threatening

letter!" George piped up. "Or are you going to blame that on Rocke, too, Mr. Bergère?"

"No, I did it. But it was his idea."

The officers stepped up to handcuff him.

"You can't do anything to me!" Bergère shouted. "I'm an American citizen!"

"But you have committed a serious crime in our country," one of the policemen told him. "We shall arrest you and try you for theft!" With that they led him away.

Madame Chambray, meanwhile, went over to Cody and kissed him on both cheeks.

"I am so pleased to meet you," she said warmly. "I have something that belongs to you—or rather Nancy does."

The girl detective pulled the diamond and lapis lazuli cross from her skirt pocket and folded it into the Texan's hand.

"Too bad Rocke didn't drop the linen wrapping," Madame Chambray murmured. "It said, 'God protect you wherever you go.' "

Cody gazed at the gleaming cross. "Oh, but I can't keep this," he finally said. "You deserve it more than I do."

"Don't be silly," Nancy replied. "It was meant to bring luck to the Vonderlicht family."

"I know you have a date," George interrupted, "but—uh—"

160

Seeing the glint of interest in her cousin's face, Bess turned to Cody. "Our search isn't over yet, you know. We're still hunting for the treasure François—I mean Friedrich—mentioned in his will. Please stay. After all, whatever we find most likely belongs to you."

Cody smiled boyishly at George, who shifted her gaze in embarrassment. "Where should we start?" he asked.

"How would you like an old birdcage?" Bess giggled and darted behind the silk screen.

"Now I'll have to buy a bird." The cowboy laughed when he saw the cage.

Nancy stared at it openmouthed. It was a magnificent birdcage, and beneath years of tarnish was gold!

"I'm positive this is the geometric figure represented in the lace cuff!" the girl detective exclaimed.

"You think so?" Bess asked in amazement. "That never occurred to me."

Suddenly aware that the ceiling beams crossed to form open triangles like the other pattern in the cuff, Nancy scanned them slowly.

"Look!" she cried, pointing to a broken hook in one of the beams. "That's where the cage used to hang. I'm sure it was a marker of some sort."

"Here," George said, handing Nancy a chair

which she placed directly under the beam and climbed up on.

"The cage must've fallen years ago," Nancy surmised. She pulled on the hook, finding it loose but unwilling to budge. Disappointed, she started to step down from the old chair, when suddenly one of the legs gave way. Nancy grabbed for the hook, desperate to find something to help her regain her balance. The small section of wood tore away from the ceiling, and Nancy toppled to the floor while the onlookers attempted to break her fall. As they bent down to help Nancy to her feet, Bess noticed a ruby-studded pin and necklace on the floor. Looking up at the hole, Bess exclaimed, "François's fortune!"

"And yours now, Cody!" Nancy added as she pulled over a stool that was standing in the corner, again stepping up to inspect the beam.

"Is there anything else?" George asked, helping Bess pick up the additional fallen treasures.

"I'll say there is!" Nancy cried in happiness. She produced the missing lace cuffs. "I never dreamed we'd ever find—"

Gleefully, the girl detective jumped down from the chair and displayed the long-hidden, delicate clue.

Just as in Gelder's painting, one cuff bore the figure of a birdcage under a pattern of baseless triangles and the words *Je vous aime*.

"What's the message in the other cuff?" Bess asked eagerly.

Nancy examined it closely, repeating the words out loud. "It's *Épousez moi, s'il vous plaît.*

"What does that mean?" Bess asked.

Nancy translated, "Please marry me."

"And that's precisely what François did!" George said.

"Except no one in his family or hers ever knew it. It was their secret!" Nancy declared. "Antoinette changed her name to Elaine Warrington when she left home, and I gather that after her husband's death, she moved to the States."

"But she never told anybody who she really was," Cody said. "Just look at how little I knew about her."

"Well," Bess sighed, "Antoinette—Elaine really got what she wanted—François—Friedrich!"

Her listeners laughed, then George remarked, "The ending of your story, Nancy, was a bit different. This turned out to be a double surprise!"

"But that's because the beginning wasn't accurate," Bess pointed out. "Your hunch about François's move to Brugge, though, was right on target!"

As she spoke, Madame Chambray sailed cheerfully into the room. She blinked tearfully when she saw the jewelry and money. "I can't believe it. You found all this?"

Cody slipped his arm around her shoulder. "Please pick out something—anything—from here you would like to keep," he said to each one.

"Oh, we couldn't," George said.

"But I insist," the young man replied. "It would make me very happy."

Reluctantly, George selected a plain but beautiful gold necklace. Cody smiled.

"I would have chosen the same thing for you," he said, causing a flush of red to spread along George's neck.

"Thank you," she murmured.

Bess decided on an old-fashioned bracelet, while Madame Chambray selected an enamel and gold pin. When Nancy's turn came, she picked a delicate chain with a beautiful locket on it. Inside were two photographs. She used her magnifying glass to decipher the faded wording underneath them.

"These are pictures of Friedrich Vonderlicht and his bride," she said. "I can't take this. Cody, you must save it for someone special."

The cowboy shifted from one foot to the other. "Then you choose something else," he said.

Nancy settled on a ruby ring. "Red will always remind me of François's jacket." She chuckled.

Madame Chambray, in the meantime, spoke quietly with Cody concerning arrangements to pick up his family possessions.

164

"Do you realize," George turned to Nancy, "that the mystery is no longer a mystery?"

"Yes, I do, if you mean the mystery about François. But what about my manuscript?" Nancy replied. "I've got to talk to Dad about it."

When she telephoned the Drew home later that day, Hannah Gruen answered. Mr. Drew was out of town, she said.

"What's your news?" Hannah asked the girl detective.

Nancy related what had happened during recent days. "It seems that Matey Johnson heard enough of our conversation to trigger off a lot of interest in Madame Chambray's letter. Then his pal intercepted my manuscript to keep me from flying to Belgium. Can you imagine that?"

"I can." The housekeeper laughed. "Of course, he didn't realize that no one can keep you from doing anything you want to."

The next day Hilda and her parents gave a farewell party for the young sleuths and their hostess, Madame Chambray. Cody and Joseph were also present.

"Can't I convince you to stay longer?" the woman asked the girls.

"I'd love to," Bess said, trying hard not to glance at Joseph who hovered near Hilda.

"So would I," George admitted, "but Nancy—"

"My tour doesn't finish for a whole week," Cody interrupted. "Why don't you change your mind?"

Nancy winked at her friends. "Well, I would like to see Ned before the summer is completely over," she said.

Now Dr. Permeke offered a toast to his guests. "It is amazing to think that such an old, old mystery has been solved," he began, "but that it took three American girls to do it—ah—that's even more wonderful!"

"And we loved every minute of it!" Nancy answered. "Thank you very much for all of your help!"

The following day the girls flew back to New York, then on to River Heights. Mr. Drew and Hannah had just greeted Nancy when the phone rang.

"I'm sure it's for you, dear," Mr. Drew told his daughter.

To her surprise, the caller was John Miller, the editor-in-chief of *Circle and Square* magazine. "So you're home," he said. "Well, I have some wonderful news for our girl detective. You won first prize in the contest!"

Nancy was almost breathless. "I did?"

"Yes. I received word from the Belgian police last night that Herbert Rocke was arrested at Brussels airport when he tried to fly back to the

States." He paused. "I sincerely regret he was one of our editors and I apologize to you for—"

"That isn't necessary," Nancy interrupted. "I'm just so thrilled about the contest." She gulped back tears of happiness as she realized her immediate challenges had finally come to an end.

Where would Nancy's next adventure take her? She would find out soon when she solved *The Greek Symbol Mystery*.

"Mr. Miller," the young detective went on, "now that I've found the real solution to the puzzle would you like me to write a new ending to 'The Secret in the Old Lace'? "

"Indeed, I'll publish it!" Mr. Miller said with a chuckle. "Deep down I was sure you would solve the mystery!"

You are invited to join

THE OFFICIAL NANCY DREW™ FAN CLUB!

Be the first in your neighborhood to find out about Nancy's newest adventures in the *Nancy Drew™ Mystery Reporter,* and to receive your official membership card. Just send your name, age, address, and zip code to:

**The Official Nancy Drew™ Fan Club**
**Wanderer Books**
**1230 Avenue of the Americas**
**New York, NY 10020**

# Don't Miss

NANCY DREW MYSTERY STORIES®
by Carolyn Keene

The Triple Hoax #57

The Flying Saucer Mystery #58

THE HARDY BOYS™ MYSTERY STORIES
by Franklin W. Dixon

Night of the Werewolf #59

Mystery of the Samurai Sword #60

The Pentagon Spy #61

The Apeman's Secret #62

The Mummy Case #63

Mystery of Smugglers Cove #64

## Plus solve-it-yourself mysteries

The Hardy Boys™ Who-Dunnit Book
by Franklin W. Dixon

Nancy Drew® Book of Hidden Clues
by Carolyn Keene

## And get your very own

My Nancy Drew® Date Book and
Homework Planner
My Nancy Drew® Private Eye Diary
complete with lock and key